THE DIRK THRUSTER JOURNALS

VOLUME 1

COLE BRADDOCK

KNOTTED ROAD PRESS

The Dirk Thruster Journals
Volume 1
Copyright © 2021 Cole Braddock
All rights reserved
Published by Knotted Road Press
www.KnottedRoadPress.com

ISBN:
978-1-64470-223-9

Cover art:
ID 50061411 © | DepositPhotos.com

NASA Nebulas

Cover and interior design copyright © 2021 Knotted Road Press

Reviews
It's true. Reviews help. Even a short one, such as, "Loved it!" So please consider reviewing this book (and all of the ones you've read) on your favorite retailer site.

Never miss a release!
If you'd like to be notified of new releases, sign up for my newsletter.

http://www.colebraddock.com/newsletter/

This book is licensed for your personal enjoyment only. All rights reserved. This is a work of fiction. All characters and events portrayed in this book are fictional, and any resemblance to real people or incidents is purely coincidental. This book, or parts thereof, may not be reproduced in any form without permission.

CONTENTS

DIRK'S SECRET MISSION

SENIOR DEPUTY TIFFANY McGee entered the bar and looked around surreptitiously as she casually made her way to one of the empty standing tables. The place was only about half full currently, in that late afternoon stretch when people might be thinking about heading back to the office to check in before going home, but before the happy hour crowd cycled in. Hanging from the ceiling, a mirrored ball reflected colored light throughout the bar, pulsing in time to the low, heavy music—Music felt more in the body than the ears.

The sex show on the small stage in the corner wasn't all that impressive. Almost desultory. Nothing that would arouse her. A man and woman, both Human, currently going at it doggy-style, but the loud music covered any sounds she was making. Although from the look on the woman's face, they wouldn't be ecstatic anyway.

As a Senior Deputy of the Amaull Timocracy, she was obviously undercover here, dressed down as slutty as she needed to be to not arouse suspicion from the locals, but not so far that anyone mistook her for one of the working girls. Fashionable yellow jumpsuit, buttoned only to her navel with no shirt under it, relying for now on boob tape to keep from showing off more than anyone in here was normally allowed to see.

The yellow went well with her straight red hair, bobbed to shoulder length and poofy when she needed to distract someone with a hair toss and a giggle. Freckles dotted her face and continued down to the visible portions of her pale breasts. White boots completed the look, marking her somewhere above the kind of girls in here who might charge in fifteen minute blocks, but not one of the office drones trolling for Mr. Right.

Or even Mr. Right-Now.

Her sharp blue eyes focused on a blond man, seated across the way in a conversation pit and nursing a beer. He hadn't noticed her come in, or if he had he was studiously ignoring her right now, probably hoping she would just vanish if he wished hard enough.

Tiffany grinned and keyed an order into the auto-bar on the table as she leaned her slender weight against it.

The crowd was better than half Human, at first glance, although that was always a hard guess, when Humans might paint themselves all manner of colors and others might disguise themselves as locals. Hazeldale Ground, below them, was a Human planet, at least these days.

A robot bartender began rolling her way, beeping quietly, but another being stepped close enough to lean on her table with a mug of something in one hand and fixed her with a winning smile.

What he probably thought was winning, anyway. Tiffany couldn't be sure, but he seemed convinced, so she was willing to let it slide.

Human, at least to the first glance. Tall and lean with skin a few degrees darker than hers but still a well-tanned Anglo. He almost reminded her of a tennis pro. Dark brown hair on his head and sideburns, parted and feathered expertly. Crossover tunic like a half-kimono in mustard silk, with brown pants a little too tight. Either he had no hair on his chest, or regularly waxed it off. Tiffany almost suggested he get some transplants, but looking at his face it was obvious that he spent more time on his makeup and skincare routine in the morning than even her little sister Tabitha, which was saying something.

"Buy a sexy little woman like you a drink?" he asked in a suave, commanding voice.

Tiffany smiled up at the man, noting that he was indeed taller than her by perhaps half a head.

"That would be polite, but it might lead you to the wrong conclusions," she cooed at him. "After all, you present as Human and male, so that might make things awkward later."

"Awkward?" he asked, suddenly a lot less convinced that he might be winning. His brown eyes registered concern.

"You don't appear to have enough places for all my penises at once," Tiffany smiled. "I'd hate to spray a mess all over you when I orgasmed. It's rude, unless you're into that sort of thing."

"But you're a girl?" he sputtered in a confused voice.

"Silly, I'm Urlik," Tiffany lied readily. "My kind are all

things. You'd need to bring several friends along if they were all Human. But that might be fun, too."

She kept the prim, inviting smile on her face as the man paled, stammered something unintelligible, and staggered off.

"Bring some friends," she called cheerfully at his back, but he wasn't stopping.

Instead, Tiffany watched him head right out the door instead, slowing only long enough to put his mug down on the end of the bar before he vanished.

She shrugged as the robot began pouring her a glass. Tiffany handed it her credit chit and left a nice tip before it went on to the next group.

Nobody ever paid attention to the automatons, forgetting that they had enough intelligence to do their job, and that meant that you could recruit them. At least a Senior Deputy of the Amaull Timocracy undercover could. Even this far from home. She might never return to Hazeldale, but she'd be in his memory banks if she did.

Tiffany took a quick sip and glanced over the crowd, once more tracking her target. Most of the rest of the beings in here were either ignoring her or had heard her claim to be an Urlik and didn't necessarily want to expand their sexual horizons that broadly. Which was probably their loss. She'd had quite an adventurous time with one on one of her missions. Three penises could be rather fun when you were ambidextrous and didn't have a gag reflex.

She smiled and grabbed her drink, sauntering her way over to the conversation pit side of the big room, letting the beat work its way down into the subsonic, where it started caressing her clitoris gently as she got closer.

Probably as intended. Certainly it was reaching inside her right now in a good way.

This space was arranged as three lobes like a clover from a central opening, solid backs all the way around and broken up with potted plants and loud music.

Tiffany came around a corner and noted that her target had his eyes closed, and was leaning back while the brunette who knelt in front of him worked his cock with both hands and her mouth. It was an impressive cock, and the woman was either enjoying his length and girth, or he'd paid her enough for the extra enthusiasm.

Tiffany slipped into the circular booth with the two of them, though not too close, and rolled a little onto her side to watch the woman's technique. His glans were in her mouth while she worked the flesh of his shaft with both hands, fast enough that she could hear the man's breath start to catch.

The woman glanced up at her now, but Tiffany motioned for her to keep working. Far be it for her to interrupt as the man seemed about to blow.

The woman winked and went back to work, humming and moaning a little herself now.

His eyes finally opened and he glanced over at her, but Tiffany didn't think he really saw anything except her cleavage. Just for the hell of it she carefully peeled the boob tape loose and pulled both breasts out for him to stare at. She wasn't close enough for the man to grasp one of them, but he didn't seem coordinated enough right now to even move.

The woman on the floor seemed to appreciate the help, though, as she started pumping his cock faster now.

And sucking harder from the way he abruptly groaned, and his eyes rolled completely back in his head. His cock started to thicken as he got close to erupting.

Tiffany found this show far more interesting than the go-go fuckers. Her breath caught a little as she remembered being in that same position, milking that lovely cock on more than one occasion. If she wasn't here on business, she might have even laid back now and fingered herself while she watched the other woman go at it. Certainly, she'd probably need to at some point.

Tiffany rated Rico a solid eight on a ten-point scale. Blond hair, long and feathered back. Chiseled abs without any massive upper body development. He always reminded her of a surfer. Tall and hunky. And nicely hung.

She watched his breath catch and his whole body spasmed. Once. Twice. A third time.

The woman sucking was managing to swallow it all as he erupted in her mouth. She must be a pro, because Tiffany remembered how much cum that man could generate when everything went just right. The feel of it dripping down her chin before she could catch it all. The bright taste.

The woman paused with her hands now, just deep throating that lovely cock and placing her palms flat on his thighs as he twitched and moaned.

Tiffany considered slipping a hand into her jumpsuit anyway, just to deal with the wetness that had developed, watching such a show and listening to the music, but she was on a mission. She could always reward herself later. Rico would be a while before he could cum again, after all, but she might need to take advantage of that, getting him hard and numb so she could just ride him for a while.

"Thank you," Rico whispered down to the woman.

No money changed hands, so Tiffany figured he'd paid up front. Or maybe she'd paid him. Rico Slade had a hell of a cock. Some women just might want to treat it like an ice cream cone.

Tiffany had, on previous missions.

The brunette rose and turned to smile at Tiffany, handing her a business card before she headed off to the rest room, presumably to fix her makeup. Or maybe inviting Tiffany for a quick snog alone.

If her mission wasn't so important, Tiffany might have even considered it. And might still, depending on what Rico had to say when he recovered.

She pulled her jumpsuit back to normal and carefully reattached the tape to her sensitive nipples, aware of how nice Rico could be in bed. Anywhere else, and he would be top stud in any room, but destiny had turned him into Dirk's mechanic, and an eleven like Dirk Thruster made even a hottie like Rico Slade look like a four by comparison.

Rico's eyes opened finally, tightly squinting against the soft overhead lighting. He turned his head and focused on her. Mostly focused.

"I thought I might be delusional," he murmured. "Lost in a wet dream, except that you were hanging just out of reach instead of straddling my face."

"It's nice to see you, too, Rico." Tiffany smiled at him as he finally moved enough to tuck that cock away.

Not that she hadn't considered bending down and

giving it a kiss while it was out. That sort of thing was only polite, right?

"Am I going to like why you're here?" Rico asked, sitting up now and grabbing a mug of something blue from where he'd put it on the shelf behind him while he got an expert blow job.

And it was expert. Tiffany'd seen and done enough of them to judge.

But she shrugged.

"I need Dirk," she said simply, causing him to chuckle.

"Every woman needs Dirk," he replied sarcastically. "That's why I hang out in dives like this where he wouldn't go, because he always immediately sucks all the oxygen and sex out of the room when he walks in."

"Do you know where he is?" Tiffany got serious.

More serious. She slipped closer now, still stretched out on her side so her covered breasts were pointed at him. Rico took a drink and tilted his head back, watching her now in the mirrored ceiling.

"It's still Wednesday, right?" Rico asked. "Hard to keep track on a station."

"It is," Tiffany replied, sipping at her own drink and watching the man recover.

Must have been one hell of a blow job. Maybe she needed to look the woman up later for her own session.

"The Tournament was supposed to be over mid-day, planetside," Rico grumbled. "Followed by an awards banquet, invitation-only drinking and sex party, and then whatever else Dirk got up to before I radioed him that the ship was finally fixed."

"Is he competing?" Tiffany asked.

That hadn't been in her briefing. She would have liked to see the man in action. Dirk Thruster was an expert in close combat, trained by many of the same people who had trained her.

But Dirk had also gotten special training later, once you had a high enough security clearance to know these things. And on top of everything else, he was a Fourth Degree Tantric Black Belt.

They said the scale went to Eight, but Dirk had never talked about his other training, according to everything Tiffany had been told.

"He's a celebrity judge," Rico replied, still staring up.

Tiffany wondered if her cleavage looked better from there, so she rolled just enough to maybe show him a better view in the reflection.

"Why does the Amaull Timocracy need Dirk this time?" Rico finally asked.

She looked around quickly, but they were alone. In the mirror overhead, there weren't even people close in the other lobes of the clover-shaped pit to listen to, but she still slid close enough to Rico to whisper in his ear. And maybe press one breast against his arm.

"The Princess is on the warpath again," she said.

He shuddered once and turned to look at her, close enough to kiss without much movement.

"Shit," Rico muttered. "So much for dragging you back to my room and having my way with you for several hours."

Tiffany kept the disappointment out of her eyes.

"Rain check?" she asked instead.

"Very funny," he said.

Tiffany caught the unintended double entendre as she leaned back. Princess Rayne of Texas. Whoops.

"Not like that," she grinned, leaning in to kiss him on the cheek anyway. And nibble on his ear.

Rico sighed and made to stand up.

"Let's go find the man," he said. "If Princess Rayne is back, he needs to know."

DIRK STUDIED Stella as she emerged from the bathroom, nude but for a barely-there robe left open. The lights in the bedroom were low. If he squinted just right, she looked remarkably like his old friend Inferno Blue. In all the good ways, too.

Chinese ancestry in the bones of her face and the tone of her skin. Mostly hairless, or perhaps so fine as to be invisible until you kissed it. Small, upturned breasts like you got with any serious martial artists, where they worked too hard and ate too carefully to really develop curves. At least until they stopped competing professionally and just taught for a living.

That was really when they turned into women, at least to his eye. Until then, it was hard to tell if a woman was sixteen or thirty.

She stepped closer, perhaps a little awkward and nervous, but Dirk wasn't surprised. He had a reputation as a lady-killer, after all. Fairly earned, but intimidating to most women. And most men.

Stella was twenty-seven. He'd triple-checked, when it became obvious that he'd kind of talked himself into being the grand prize for the woman, after she won in her weight category. She could still pass for sixteen in the right light. Petite and lean, barely five feet tall and one hundred fifteen pounds of whipcord and muscle. Had they allowed it, she might have won against the heavyweight champion as well. She was that good.

Dirk was on the bed, stretched out and leaning against a pile of pillows. The pearl-colored sheets, so bright against the darker tones of his skin and black body hair, were drawn negligently across his midsection in a way that looked accidental. It was not. He'd had too much training in such things for anything in a bedroom to be an accident.

Some days, that took all the fun out of it. Howie had warned him about that, but Dirk had mostly been able to avoid it. Maybe he was just feeling morose tonight. Or this was the emotional letdown after a good tournament.

When even the thought of sex gets a little stale…

But then he took a good look at her nudity. At her labia peeking out from the tiny triangle of hair between her legs, possibly already glistening with arousal. That little hint of nervousness that made her seem a little vulnerable right now, standing there like a statue of perfection.

Dirk knew he needed to take extra special care of this woman. Live up to the legend that had been built around the name Dirk Thruster. At the same time, he found himself looking forward to all the places he might touch her. Taste her. Pleasure her. He had a vision of a violin, awaiting his touch in an empty auditorium that he could fill with the sounds of her orgasm.

It was a lie that he could cause a woman to have an

orgasm just by looking at her across the room, but that legend might certainly contribute to making it easier for some of the ones he had known to get off quickly. And he did enjoy the effect a simple smile had on many women.

Especially this one. Hot, hard, compact, gorgeous. His soft cock awoke with a twitch, like a snake sensing movement nearby and started to lengthen as he stared at her.

Dirk held out a hand and Stella took it, shrugging out of the robe to stand proudly nude before him now. And maybe a little nervous about climbing into bed with Dirk Thruster and his legendary cock.

Dirk pulled her into a kiss, then let her settle, wrapped up against him and pressed tight while he ran a hand down her back and explored the muscles there and in her bottom.

It was an amazing bottom. That was what had originally drawn his eye. Her technique was impeccable, but that ass was something to write home about. Touching it, he knew that first glance had been correct. Dirk almost wanted to make a new hobby of bouncing coins off of it.

Visually, they were almost polar opposites as he studied the woman. He was tall, dark, and hairy, with a thick, dark, wavy mane and hair on his chest so heavy it was almost a pelt. He kept the chin clean, most of the time, cultivating a mustache instead that dropped a little past the corners of his mouth in such a way that his smile seemed to have that much more impact.

He was fully hard now, smelling her. One of Stella's hands tentatively reached out and she wrapped her fingers around his shaft as he kissed the top of her head and played with her bottom. His other hand moved into the mix and began to just rub a light friction across one of her nipples. Not much, because they were already so hard they might cut glass, but enough to take her gasp suddenly. He considered leaning down to kiss one, but worried she might cum just from that, as wound up as the woman appeared to be.

There was no rush to what he intended to do to this woman. Hell, he still hadn't gotten a message from Rico that the ship had been fixed from the latest breakdown, so he could take hours and enjoy everything that fate had cast up into his lap today in the form of Stella.

Slow, languid, everything fun.

She looked up now and he kissed her, shifting things around until they were side by side with his right arm up. Her free arm came up around his neck and held the kiss while he worked her bottom, alternatively kneading the muscles and lightly stroking the flesh down to the backs of her knees.

Howie had instructed him on all the correct techniques. Touch her here. Kiss her there, there, and there. Prod her this way. Squeeze just so. Stroke across here, but only as light as if you were touching a razor blade.

Had he wanted, Dirk could have already taken her into a series of mind-shattering orgasms in seconds, but that sounded too much like work. He wasn't on a mission, needing to seduce a target.

Stella had shyly asked if he was the grand prize. There had been a lot of drinking and camaraderie going on, so he'd said sure. What was the worst that could have happened, after all? He didn't get laid tonight?

Dirk slipped down her body a little, his cock now too far away for her hands to continue caressing it, but that was fine. They had all night. Instead, he kissed her just below the ear, feeling her whole body tense beneath him as she sucked a hard breath in, pressing her nipples against his chest.

He moved a little lower now and closer to the front of her neck, licking and nibbling as he looked for all the right places. He must have found one, because she started to purr and writhe against him. Dirk shifted his weight onto his left elbow so his right hand was free to continue tracing her skin lightly down her ribs, goosebumps standing up now wherever he went.

Her right nipple was next for a quick kiss. They were such perfect nipples. He ran his tongue over it a few times and then sucked lightly, feeling her back arch with a tiny whimper as he started to pull away. On to the other nipple now, lest it get jealous. Hell, he could possibly spend days at this, as sensitive as they seemed to be. It might turn into a hobby, if he was going to be spending more time on this planet. Or wherever she lived.

Dirk shifted up onto his knees and elbow so he could reach a hand under her back and down her bottom, lifting the leg into the air as he traced his way around between then, never touching anyplace sensitive, but heightening all the nerves as he did.

She smelled lovely after a quick shower with floral soap, but it was competing with her sudden musk, filling the air with need and desire. Dirk kept moving south as he kissed her, pausing to let his tongue lap circles around her belly button. He pressed her legs flat as he worked, spreading them out enough that he could trace her labia up and down with a finger, pausing at the top at her clitoris and then the bottom, just resting on her anus, but not pressing.

Maybe later, if she needed something like that to make her brain explode.

He turned now and slipped his head between her legs, pausing just to enjoy her smell before he leaned in and kissed her clit. One of her hands found his cock, now that it was close again, and started to work the flesh up and down with a firm grip used to holding a sparring sword. Or a bō.

She tasted sweet. And gasped when his tongue penetrated her pussy the first time. Tart, like a freshly-cut apple. That was the benefit of a woman in such amazing shape. She exercised constantly and ate well, so her pussy was like ambrosia.

Dirk lapped at the nectar of the gods themselves and thought about how lucky he was in life.

He paused, looking up at her now as his cock was starting to tingle a little from what she was doing. Good, but he wasn't ready to be done with her.

"What?" she gasped, still gripping his cock like a life preserver.

From the look in his eyes, she'd slide right under him in a sixty-nine if he moved at all, but Dirk had more interesting things in mind. And didn't want to peak without enjoying her more. There were times when a quickie was good, but this wasn't one of them, as much fun as it might be.

He wanted to truly savor this woman.

"I'm going to have you for dessert," he smiled up at her and shifted, climbing off the edge of the bed and tugging at her to move.

Stella took a moment to grasp, and then turned. Dirk reached down and more or less lifted her to the edge of the bed before he knelt, resting her thighs on his shoulders and reaching up to cup each small breast as he began to kiss her.

Yes, this was the best part, when a woman relaxed and opened herself up to you. There were so many things he wanted to do to explore this woman, but first things first, he wanted to taste her. Drink that tart nectar in and enjoy himself almost as much as she was.

Her clitoris seemed to be begging for attention now, so Dirk wrapped his lips around it and began to suck lightly. It was like someone had passed an electric current through her body from the way she went rigid under him and began to rock. Down below, he stayed hard as a rock, just from the sounds of her enjoying this. He released the suction and ran his tongue up and down her pussy now, drinking in the immense wetness as she tried to squeeze his head with her legs.

He let go of one of her breasts and slipped a hand under Stella as he returned to her clit, pressing his index finger slowly into her pussy, feeling her muscles try to milk it. Once it was moist, he withdrew the digit and just rested it against her anus for a moment, tapping in rhythm with his lips on her clitoris.

She was starting to thrash now, spasming as he worked faster and a little rougher. His finger penetrated her ass, but only to the first knuckle. More wasn't needed, because her first orgasm hit with a scream that might have rivaled the fire alarm. He wondered if he might actually be able to orgasm, just from the sound of her cumming her brains out and grinding herself against his mouth. Might be fun to find out sometime.

Dirk tugged lightly at her nipple with his other hand, not pinching so much as pulling upright, and using that arm to keep her from bucking him off. Her orgasm stretched, surging and receding.

He wasn't sure if what happened next should be counted as one long orgasm, three big ones, or seven little ones. The moaning, gasping, and bucking went on for nearly a minute before she finally reached down and pulled at his hair to stop.

Yeah, that reaction from a woman was one of the best things in life.

Dirk leaned back finally, withdrawing his finger from her ass slowly and carefully. He kissed the inside of both thighs and then softly right on her wet pussy. Standing, he rolled Stella onto her side as she curled up in a fetal position.

"Be right back," he said as he pulled the sheet over her quivering body.

Dirk smiled at himself in the mirror as he washed his hands and splashed his face. Whatever else you wanted to say, that always left him feeling like a god.

And he hadn't even cum yet.

Dirk slipped into bed and curled himself around her,

cupping one breast with a hand and slipping the other arm under her head. Stella purred contentedly, but he wasn't sure she hadn't passed out there for a minute.

Truly, godlike.

He smiled and kissed the back of an ear, feeling her heart slowing down and her breath returning to normal.

Time passed. She might have fallen asleep. His cock relaxed as he fell into a meditation, no longer prodding at her backside.

Stella awoke with a jolt that was almost comical. She rolled over inside his arms and looked up at his in worried surprise.

"You didn't get to," she whispered, frantic.

"You were in no position," he assured her, pulling her close and pressing her against his chest.

"No," she agreed. "I might have passed out."

"You did," he nodded, leaning down to kiss her, tongues dancing as she began to moan again.

"You never even fucked me, Dirk," she said. "I need your cock now."

"We can arrange something."

Rather than answer, she slid down the bed and took him in her mouth, pulling it straight with one hand and licking at it as it hardened again.

"It's so huge," she whispered before slipping the tip into her mouth.

Dirk watched her suck greedily on his cock, his eyes threatening to roll back in his head at her expert technique.

Too big was a bad thing, he'd learned early on. If you had too much cock, not many women could wrap their mouth around it, and stretching their vagina to take it all ended up being so painful they weren't enjoying themselves, which tended to sour things for him.

He had eight inches of length, but the girth was such that Stella could barely get her petite hands all the way around it. Two inches across the shaft, a little wider at the head.

But she was intent. Hungry, even. Apparently, the woman had a gag reflex, so she didn't try to take it all, but bobbed on the tip with her tongue like that ridge of muscle just inside the pussy. The one that provides all the right friction on the frenulum.

She got him hard and wet and then looked up in anticipation.

"I need all of you inside me," she said with a hungry smile.

He rolled her flat and slipped a finger slowly inside her, letting her muscles relax and grip it. A second finger followed a moment later, stretching her sideways. Dirk curled his fingers a little and found her g-spot. It was like flipping a light switch on and off, looking in her eyes. He got even harder, if that was possible, just staring into those eyes

"Please fuck me," Stella whimpered as her pussy got even wetter.

Dirk climbed between her legs and knelt there, holding his cock in one hand and rubbing it up and down her labia slowly as she squirmed. He reached up and pulled one of her hands down to do the work now, rubbing herself with the tip of his cock. Her other hand came along with it and began rubbing her clit in the same rhythm.

Stella pulled her lips out of the way and tugged at his cock, so Dirk moved forward, pressing slowly, grinding into her wet pussy, that first stroke barely fitting the tip in. Her pussy had a grip almost as firm and lovely as she'd had with her hand early. She gasped and wriggled some more, her muscles still tense as he stretched her out.

Dirk withdrew a little and heard her moan in disappointment that turned into a gasp as he drove his hard cock into her again, a little deeper this time as her vagina muscles began to relax, allowing him deeper inside her with each stroke.

Slowly, she opened up like a flower, soaking wet now but still gripping him tight. Dirk wondered if he was splitting this petite woman in two down the middle. Still, she was an expert martial artist with extreme body control. Her pussy stretched and he buried all the way to the tip, feeling like he was just perfectly short of tapping her cervix when he was inside her.

It was glorious. Tight and wet and rubbing his whole shaft top to bottom. Most women didn't have the internal muscle tone to do something like that and Dirk knew he wouldn't last long with the way she felt.

She moaned and hooked her heels on his thighs, holding him in place as everything reshaped inside her, getting an even firmer grip on his hard cock. Her hands came up and grabbed onto his shoulder blades like a life preserver in rough seas. Dirk leaned down to kiss her on the forehead and tasted her sweat as they started to find the right rhythm.

Dirk began to pump slowly, feeling every ripple of her vaginal walls bump over the veins on his shaft. Her clitoris seemed to be standing up, pressing against him where they met and letting her grind against his tight abs. She writhed and bucked as he drove his cock into her again and again.

He leaned back a little now and paused, buried all the way to hilt in her heavenly warmth, resting his weight on his left arm while his right thumb slipped between them and found that wonderful clitoris. Stella screamed and jerked hard enough on his thighs that she might have left bruises.

Dirk shifted onto his elbows again found his rhythm. In and out. Full and empty. Moan and whimper beneath him. Hard breath as she squeezed him and rocked his world.

"More," she murmured. "Fuck me. Fill me."

He liked the sound of her voice as she started building to another orgasm. The gasps and twitches.

The need.

He felt that familiar fire slowly catch, deep in his core. His breathing changed and everything turned to white noise in his head as his whole mind had no thought now but to cum. To fill her up and let her milk him empty.

Dirk's breaths turned to rasps. Muscles everywhere coiled up like springs, so tight that it almost hurt to move, but he was past stopping. Past caring about anything except his own need and that pussy holding him, pinning him. Milking him.

"Oh, God, yes." She became even more frantic. "Fuck me harder."

He tried, pumping harder as if he was truly going to split her in two now.

She moaned when his cock thickened, like maybe her pussy had finally reached its limits. He pumped, feeling what little control he'd had left slipping away.

Dirk blasted an orgasm into her like an arrow entering flesh. One pulse. Another. A third.

Stella might have had another orgasm somewhere in the middle, but he'd lost coherence, mindlessly jackhammering her pussy as he filled her with hot cum, unable to do anything else as he lost control.

Finally, everything seized up and Dirk collapsed atop her, covered in sweat, room spinning, light far too bright, even on the lowest setting.

When the world returned to normal, he withdrew his shrinking cock, more or less fell onto his side, and then rolled onto his back still gasping for breath. Stella wasn't doing any better as she clung to his side. She might have been crying, but they appeared to be tears of joy, from the sounds she was making. Hard to tell.

Dirk focused on returning to normal as he wrapped an arm around her and pulled the sheet up. She would need a hand towel at some point. Maybe another shower. Either of them might drown if they moved too soon, though.

His breath finally fell into a rhythm. Fourth Degree Tantric Black Belts learned extreme body control, but some things were more fun when you let them run wild. Like fucking a woman as hungry and flexible as Stella. Letting everything go and leaving it all on the mat. Or on the bed.

Finally, the room stopped spinning and he stirred.

"You lay still," he said, "I'll get you a warm towel."

Dirk slipped from the bed and staggered to the bathroom, wondering how soon he could find an excuse to visit Stella's homeworld and do that again. She had been more than amazing. Epic.

Dirk wondered if he might need to go back and study for higher tantric belts, just to top what had just happened.

He ran the water bloodwarm and then wet a towel, wiping himself down, wringing it out, and then damping it again. Dirk returned to the bed and handed it to Stella, delighting as he got to just watch her lay back and slowly, carefully clean herself. From the look on her face, every skin nerve she had was overloaded right now.

He felt godlike. The best way to go through life.

After she finished, Dirk threw the towel through the bathroom door, rather than trying to move until both of them recovered more. He pulled up enough pillows to sit upright and pulled her into his lap where she curled up and purred.

For all the other things he did in this galaxy, nights like this tended to make up for it.

A beeping interrupted, causing him to stir and Stella to nearly jump out of her skin. He held her close and studied the offending sound. His handcomm chirped again.

Rico.

He considered ignoring it. Dirk was supposed to call Rico to check in tomorrow, or Rico would leave a message that the ship was ready for deep-space flight.

Calling indicated that something had gone wrong.

"I have to take this," he finally said to Stella, kissing her.

She sighed and collapsed flat beside him. After a moment, she rolled over away from him, curled up, and possibly fell instantly asleep.

Mission accomplished, indeed.

Dirk grabbed the handcomm and flipped it open.

"Better be good, Rico," he grumbled at his mechanic and best friend.

"Oh, it is," a woman answered. "It is."

It took him a moment to place the voice. Tiffany McGee. Amaull Timocracy Agent. Occasionally answered to *Tits* McGee when she was in a good mood.

"Are you holding him for ransom?" Dirk had to ask.

"Oh? Would that actually work?" she countered sarcastically, reminding him why he put up with the woman when the Timocracy needed him on those special, secret missions.

"Probably not," Dirk replied. "I could always find another mechanic."

"Hey, that's not nice," Rico said in the background.

"Why are you on Hazeldale, Tiffany?" Dirk asked bluntly.

He'd just gotten fucked utterly silly, so Dirk wasn't happy that the rest of the galaxy seemed to want to intrude.

"Looking for you, Dirk," she said, stating the obvious. "We need to meet and talk in private."

He looked over at Stella, purring quietly as she snored.

"I'm not alone," he said. "But if you talk quietly, you won't wake her."

"We have a report that Princess Rayne is on the move again, Dirk," McGee said simply. "Our sources think she might have actually found a way to penetrate the Forbidden Triangle."

Well, shit.

Two minutes ago, he would have sworn that there was nothing his old friends at the Amaull Timocracy could have said right now that would cause him to do another mission for them. Not after last time.

He'd have been wrong, too.

"How time critical is this information?" he finally asked.

"I'm sitting on your bridge with Rico," Tiffany replied. "Is that enough?"

Dirk sighed.

"Have someone downstairs at my hotel in thirty minutes," he decided. "I need a shower, and then I suppose I have to go save the universe again, don't I?"

Dirk cut the line rather than wait for a reply. She wouldn't say anything he wanted to hear.

He leaned over to kiss Stella on the ear, but she rolled back to kiss him back.

"You heard?" he said after a moment.

"Enough," she nodded with a half-smile. "Back to duty for the legendary Dirk Thruster?"

"Something like that," he agreed. "Otherwise, I might have you for first breakfast in a few hours, too."

She pouted for a moment and then grinned at him.

Dirk returned the smile and untangled himself from her to slide from the bed and stretch.

He smiled down at the woman, taking an extra

moment to ogle her perfect nudity. Sculptors working in stone would likely throw down their tools in disgust at being unable replicate such beauty.

He wasn't even remotely ready to settle down anywhere, but she was the sort of woman that would still haunt him from time to time.

"Need someone to wash your back?" she grinned.

"Best be quick."

DIRK SIGHED as the space taxi brought him into the dock on *Longsword,* his armed scout that Rico had turned into a fast gunship. It had one of the fastest deep-space drives known to experimental science, but those things also tended to be fragile.

For Dirk, that extra eight percent of speed he had on everyone else was worth the trouble, even as much time as they had to spend occasionally limping into port to repair something that had cooked when he'd ridden them too hard.

When everything aligned, though, there was nobody in the galaxy that could keep up.

He smiled and waved at the driver as she backed away from the dock. Dirk had left a nice tip with the pilot and even signed the woman's log book as proof she'd really flown Dirk Thruster himself around when he was on Hazeldale. Probably worth free drinks with all her girlfriends, although he wondered how soon the story would morph into a wild sexcapade where she'd set the autopilot for the climb out of gravity and then they'd fucked in every position possible in zero gravity until docking.

Dirk figured that he'd only done about half the things people claimed about him. Fortunately, the pieces they would pick for fables tended to be the ones that actually happened, and the mundane stuff like seducing a taxi driver was the outrageous part.

Not that she'd been ugly. A few pounds heavy, but they didn't all have to be built like Stella. Even that perfection would drive a man to boredom pretty quickly, like having oatmeal for breakfast every morning.

That just wasn't Dirk's style.

The inner lock opened and Dirk stepped back onto his own deck finally. The hydroponics section had an entire wing dedicated to the flowers that Rico liked to grow, although he'd rarely own up to it. But it gave the entire ship a scent of roses and springtime that you never got anywhere else.

Dirk had considered suggesting it to a few of the stations he'd visited, but why give up any edge he didn't have to? Every woman that stepped into his life support envelope smelled it, got seduced by it, but few understood what it was.

Still, it relaxed them in all the important ways.

The *Longsword* was long and slender, as befit a scout turned gunship. Two big engine pods aft to drive them. Cargo bays as well, where the ship had been stretched and widened to suit Dirk's needs, plus more space along the shaft headed forward. Life support in the middle of the vessel, with bridge, quarters, and entertainment spaces forward where the hull belled out some before coming down to a blunt point.

He turned left and headed forward, automatically checking things as he went.

Rico was on the bridge when he got there. Senior Deputy Tiffany "Tits" McGee was seated in a passenger chair rather than at his station, which was good. There were limits to how far he'd let the woman push.

Even Tiffany.

She was still gorgeous. Deadly-blue eyes studied him as he entered and turned his chair around to watch her as he sat. Auburn-red hair, full and wavy, thick enough to grab a fistful and pull.

Her freckles were so faint as to be almost invisible, but he didn't know if that meant that she'd been spending too much time indoors, or had added a layer of foundation to her otherwise flawless, porcelain-white skin to hide them.

She wasn't wearing a necklace, so he was able to trace a single line from her chin all the way to her belly button. There'd been a few times where he'd done that with wine.

"What do we know?" he began.

"You haven't even said yes yet, Dirk," she teased, tilting her head just so and smiling that secret smile.

"Oh?" he countered. "I should make you beg a little first? Offer me all manner of inducements, personal or professional, to help out? Is that what you needed today?"

"Wouldn't want to make it too easy for you," Tiffany grinned. "It can't really be worth that much if a girls is just giving it away now, can it?"

"But you have needs," Dirk observed. "That special

thing that nobody else in the galaxy can satisfy but me, can they?"

"There's only one Dirk Thruster," Tiffany said, arching her back and neck just a little to push her breasts in his direction.

"Are you two going to fuck, or can we talk about the mission first?" Rico interrupted.

Dirk shared a grin with Tiffany before he turned to his annoyed mechanic and nodded.

"Rico's right," he said. "Let's just assume that the information you have is important enough for us to drop everything and immediately go chasing after Princess Rayne of Texas and whatever trouble she's going to cause today."

"I was having fun," Tiffany pouted.

"And if I decide that your information's not up to snuff, you'll have to be punished." Dirk smiled at her sideways.

"Gonna spank me, Dirk?" she asked in a throaty voice.

"I might get out the seven-meter cord first," he offered blandly. "Shibari you into an art installation, where you can't do anything but lay there and watch as we take turns."

He watched her eyes light up with lust, but he knew Tiffany. Knew her foibles. He wouldn't call them weaknesses. That suggested flaws.

Kinks, perhaps.

Her pupils dilated as he studied her.

"Or Rico and I might bind you properly, and then sit down with a bottle of wine and spend the night playing backgammon," he continued, just to watch her deflate a little.

Maybe squirm a little, too.

"So what is the princess up to?" Dirk turned serious finally.

Tiffany took a deep breath to regain her composure before she spoke.

"Our spies intercepted a message that suggests she might have found a way to penetrate the Forbidden Triangle," Tiffany said.

Dirk leaned back and considered the implications.

The Forbidden Triangle was a three-sided zone of space covering nearly two whole sectors where deep-space drives simply didn't work. It was like someone had built an energy barrier, several hundred light-years on a side.

Any vessel encountering the barrier was immediately destroyed, so everyone gave it a wide berth.

At the same time, rumors suggested a number of powerful worlds hidden on the inside. Godlike beings, ancient and dangerous, who had built those unexplainable walls to keep out the barbarians that had come along in the last few thousand years.

Nobody knew. That was the clincher. It could be anything, from true gods all the way down to some bizarre natural phenomenon based on a quirk of interstellar physics that might pop one day like a soap bubble.

He studied Tiffany now, professionally.

"And Dr. Regulus sent you?" he asked.

"I was closest, when the message went out. And I've worked with you in the past."

"What does Regulus and the rest of The Synod think

will happen if she get manages to access the Forbidden Triangle?" Dirk pressed.

"We don't know," she admitted. "That was why they apparently decided that you should be brought in immediately. You'd do the right thing. And you have a history of thwarting Rayne, if she does find something so dangerous that she threatens the galaxy, instead of just dreaming about it."

Dirk grimaced. All of that was true. He had and he would. Princess Rayne was a spoiled girl, given too much power and latitude by her impossibly wealthy father, King Zerik. Not truly evil, but headstrong and unwilling to listen when someone told her no.

"Do we at least know where we're going?" Dirk asked.

"Dr'Gonai," Tiffany said carefully, as if she was afraid he might bite her.

Or refuse.

"Dr'Gonai," he echoed.

At least she had the decency to flinch a little, as if commiserating with his pain. Not that she could. Not that anyone could. Anybody else besides the princess causing grief and he might indeed refuse, but nobody else could stop that woman when she was on the hunt.

They were all going to end up owing him for this one. Best be about it, then.

"I'll assume your gear is already aboard, since you kidnapped my mechanic for ransom?" Dirk glanced at the two of them.

"It is," she said carefully.

He nodded to Rico.

"Put her in the ambassadorial suite," he said simply,

ignoring her squawk of contained outrage as he turned back to his console and started bringing systems on line.

He hadn't asked her to come. Hadn't requested that the Timocracy interrupt his vacation. They could deal with him on those terms, or they could fuck right off and get someone else to do it.

Behind him, he heard them both depart, so he relaxed and started calculating a deepspace path to Dr'Gonai. There was a planet there, but almost nobody remembered that, except as a hinterland supplying fresh food and industrial machine parts for the stations in orbit.

Including the most famous starship in the galaxy: the *Jira Sleeper Ship*. Playground to the stars.

Going back there was going to suck.

TIFFANY TOOK a deep breath as Rico closed the hatch, leaving her alone in the ambassadorial suite with her two bags just inside the door.

She'd been here before, on previous missions. Usually when accompanying an actual ambassador, though. This was Dirk's blunt way to establish boundaries on this mission. She'd hoped he might put her in the third crew cabin forward, located between the two of them and immediately accessible to either.

Not that she could argue with his overall anger. The Timocracy had dealt him a bad hand last time, then thrown a fit when he'd made the best of it, but still fallen short of the impossible task that they had just taken for granted.

But she had hoped…

Now was not the time to plead her case, and she knew it. She grabbed both bags and shifted them out of the main room and into the oversized bedroom, stopping to peek into the bathroom with the tub that could hold an orgy of six if you were careful and dried everything down afterwards.

She'd been up and running for too many hours, so Tiffany just flopped onto her back on the edge of the bed with her feet on the floor, not even turning the lights on.

It had been a crapshoot that Dirk would even listen. Any other agent might have just been tossed out onto the dock and left there to rot when Dirk and his *Longsword* left, so she counted everything until now as a win.

At the same time, the air both here and on the station had been heavy with the musk of desire and the funk of hot, fresh sex. Watching Rico get his cock milked by another woman had left her damp. Seeing Dirk again just ignited something in her belly.

But the man wasn't going to quench it anytime soon. His eyes had said that much. Rico might be willing, but then again, he might not. The lights were down. She was alone. She'd just have to take care of herself.

One hand slipped inside her open jumpsuit now and gingerly peeled the tape. She'd been wearing it too long again, and her nipples were starting to chafe. She'd have to wear nothing but silk across them for a few days while they recovered. Quickly, the other breast was loose, and she shrugged out of the arms of the jumpsuit.

Tiffany left the pants on for now. Removing her slippers sounded like too much work at this point as well.

Her left hand reached up to cup a breast, just kneading it lightly with a hint of a wince when she got too close to the nipple. Her left hand slipped into the bottom half of her jumpsuit and inside her panties.

She'd even gone to the spa, just before leaving home, and gotten everything waxed, leaving a cute little triangle of red fur for anyone exploring to encounter. Not a Forbidden Triangle, at least not when Dirk or Rico were around.

She already knew the ground, so she quickly trod across it and down into the chasm beyond, pausing to circle her clit once, making her breath catch.

Further down, she ran her finger into the moistness, parting her lips and pressing the top of her finger just past that little ring of muscle and then withdrawing it, time and again, imagining Dirk's tongue fucking her as she got wetter and wetter.

Deciding her nipples were just too sensitive, Tiffany let go and slid her left hand down her side and then in with her right, her middle finger penetrating deeper now as she began to work on her clit with two fingers on her left hand.

Dirk would do that to her. Rico as well, but he was just Human when he did, while Dirk was a shaman calling the lust gods down to inhabit her body with just his touch.

Her clit ached for his lips, but she made do, rubbing back and forth, faster and faster, her other hand plunging into her pussy like a cock impaling her.

Tiffany's breath grew ragged. Her back arched, driving her hips into the air as she fucked herself, wishing she were a Nicia right now, so she would have two more hands to pleasure herself, maybe drilling her ass with a dildo while the other one tangled a handful of hair and pulled hard. Like Dirk did when he felt like being nice.

She stopped breathing, every muscle pulled rigid like she had been turned to stone, as the orgasm took hold, hitting like an earthquake in the form of a lightning bolt, electrocuting every nerve ending at once.

Maybe one orgasm would have been enough, but she'd really wanted Rico's cock in her mouth when he came, back there on the station. Or to be there in the room watching when Dirk took the welterweight champion to Elysium and back.

Tiffany kept rubbing. Kept thrusting. Rode a second orgasm, just a small one, almost a placeholder, as the third one built. She jammed three fingers into her soaking pussy now, grinding on her clit with the heel of her hand, rather than just rely on pitiful fingers.

Four. FIVE. **SIX**. *seven*. Eight.

Tiffany finally remembered to breathe, just cupping her clit with one palm and her aching pussy with the other as she stopped thrashing.

Thank God she'd left the lights down. Even at sleep setting they were too bright.

But at least she'd be able to think clearly tomorrow. And not pant after Dirk or Rico as they all went in pursuit of that spoiled brat princess and whatever stupid plan she'd come up with this time.

Around her, Tiffany felt another surge of power take hold, but it was just the ship backing away from the station, like Dirk's cock withdrawing from her pussy when his task was done, and then turning towards the stars.

She'd gotten the man this far. Hopefully, she had convinced him to save the galaxy again and not be mad at her or the Timocracy.

He'd find a way to stop the princess and then finally take Tiffany to bed and give her the deep, hard fucking she really needed.

JIRA SLEEPER SHIP

DIRK STUDIED the room as he came through the door of the casino floor.

Vast.

Broken up by walls and gaming tables, shops and restaurants, spanned above the space by an impressive three-story vault overhead, with a variety of potted plants hanging on beams and climbing them like ivy to help clean the slightly-smoky air and deaden some of the sound. The dominant smell was tobacco, but there were other things floating above and below that scent. He might have complained, but in places like this that sweet tang in the air was frequently necessary to cover the smell of people sweating too much in too tight confines. Or from a few folks either putting on a public sex performance or just getting busy in a handy, shadowed recess.

Orbital resort casinos were, after all, just a filter to separate tourists from their money in the most efficient way possible. But Dirk wasn't here to gamble. Or rather, maybe just gamble with his life and his soul, rather than his cash.

He needed information, and to get it he was going to have to search through this entire mass of people to find the handful that could tell him what he needed to know.

Looking around, there were probably a thousand beings in sight right now: gaming, watching, eating, or fornicating, as the mood and need struck. The ratio seemed to be about a third Human, a third who were probably close enough to pass in the dark, and a third who covered both ends of the standard classification schema.

Warm-blooded oxygen breathers for the most part, though, with a few in bio-suits to replicate an environment different enough that they might poison others, or be poisoned themselves.

The music was a full string orchestra, likely playing that same loop of thirty or forty songs that had spread over all of Human space. Anodyne, but not prosaic. At the same time also not so energetic that folks would want to get up from their drinking or gambling to dance.

After all, if they weren't gambling, the house didn't make money. Only the bars and the barely-clad waitresses would.

All that in a glance as he followed the flow of the crowd coming out of the lift.

Somewhere on this ship was a person who knew why the princess was coming, or at least what she was looking for. He just had to make some contacts.

On his arm was Amaull Timocracy Senior Deputy Tiffany McGee, throwing enough swagger into her hips that Dirk wondered if she might dislocate something. She looked so unlike her normal self that going down on her on a particularly tasty day might be the only way you could even recognize the woman. Chemical treatments and extensions had lengthened her hair almost to her firm, ripe bottom, leaving it straight and taking it so far down the visual spectrum that it was almost true black.

And not just the hair on her head.

She'd left her breasts the same size, on the presumption that they were just right now, and not worth adjusting her wardrobe that extensively. Instead, she wore a pale blue silk wrap that danced between gown and sundress, clinging in all the right places to *suggest*, without ever *proving*.

Her skin had been dyed that particular Kelly green that a L'Quene woman strove for on a daily basis. Tiffany's blue eyes stood out from her skin like glacial diamonds.

Her own mother would not know her.

He was still Dirk Thruster, not in disguise so much as perhaps mufti. Not obviously being the Legendary Dirk Thruster™, Fourth Degree Tantric Black Belt. At least not until his name triggered quiet alarms in various systems.

He'd deal with those issues as they came.

But he had also slipped a few bills to folks along the way with a wink and a nod about the importance of secrecy. Maybe a special mission. Perhaps an assignation. Or even shooting a new action/adventure vid.

Best way to handle it all was to deny everything with an evasive twinkle in the eye and a sly smile.

He'd even left his ship, *The Longsword*, down on the surface of the planet below, where Rico could more easily acquire or build spare parts without having to worry about keeping the life support system operational all the time. That way, *The Longsword* would be available if he needed it, but wouldn't show up on any scans of orbital traffic, or on a docking registry, if someone bribed a purser.

That might be important, considering that he figured he was only a few days ahead of the arrival of *The Libertine* and its Commandtrix: the Princess Rayne of Texas. Only child of King Zerik. Spoiled beyond measure, with too much money and power, and nobody had ever been able to make a *No* stick.

She'd chased after him, more than once. And also been thwarted in various plans to take over the galaxy.

Rayne would make a terrible empress. Governing would be too much like work for her, when all she really wanted was to enjoy herself. It was a shame she tended to be so boring in bed.

Seriously? You consider reverse cowgirl a little kinky, lady?

Dirk took in the whole sweep of the room and guided their path to a semi-confined space on his left, down two half-levels as the floor in here wandered to all sorts of elevations and depressions like a wilderness had been brought to orbit and merged.

The young Human woman at the front of the bar they approached eyed him speculatively. Without even knowing who he was, Dirk watched her lick her lips once unconsciously before guiding Tiffany and him into the bar and putting them at a small table in the patio area, closed off on all sides but open above. A sound-field was active, excluding the orchestra. Instead, the music just starting up as they sat was a hard, slow grind, and the stage show was a woman slowly working a brass pole, thrusting her ass out and wiggling to the enthusiastic cheers of the audience.

Trilloo, from her coloring, her skin a lighter shade of blue than just azure, but close, and her hair was a green darker than Tiffany's new skin. Well built, too, with a wasp waist holding up a wrap in shimmering gold cloth across a flat stomach and the sorts of broad, friendly hips you grabbed with both hands when she wanted you to bend her over a table to take her.

Above all that, two large breasts strove to explode out of a top that was just a long strip of cloth tied with the simple knot resting between them.

They were obviously early in her show. The Trilloo woman hadn't phase-shifted yet, so it was just her alone on stage right now, teasing and smiling.

Dirk ordered a whiskey sour on the rocks for himself, while Tiffany got a glass of the house red. They weren't doing anything right now but keeping a low profile. No big-stakes games. No request for special treatment from the manager or the chef. Just two tourists seeing the seething, carnal pot of pleasure that was the Albrecht Casino on the *Jira Sleeper Ship*, one of the most famous vessels in space.

A Shydrun waitress quickly delivered their drink and got a good tip. Again, not large enough to be memorable, but not too small either.

Up on the stage, the Trilloo dancer was finally starting to glow. Dirk felt her eyes upon him like a searchlight across the darkness, so he toasted the woman and returned her smile. She seemed to laugh, and then closed her eyes and wrapped her arms around herself.

The glow got brighter, but not painful or harmful. Enough that she didn't need a spotlight on her anymore.

She began to separate. There was a scientific name for it. Whole branches of science that explained how it worked, but to Dirk it was all still a special kind of magic. Where they had been one woman a few moments, ago, now there were three, identically dressed. The original had been pointing her body almost at him, so Dirk hadn't seen the split, but now an identical one stepped out from behind her to the right, and another behind *her* to the left.

Still, all three seemed to be ignoring the rest of the audience to smile at Dirk. He sipped and admired them as they began to dance. It almost felt like he had a private show.

Dirk wondered what a lap dance would feel like, if there were three of them involved.

Even the finest troupe in the galaxy could not replicate the form of a Trilloo dancing, because all three of them shared one consciousness, even in separate bodies. And she was exceptional. The middle woman untied her bandeau, but held it in place, flashing bits of cleavage without showing any more.

On the left, that version had untied her wrap around her thighs while she held the cloth in place across her center, showing a flash of long, powerful thigh as she moved and distracting you to look close enough to see heaven.

The third version of the dancer moved behind the first, wrapping her hands across the woman's waist and then up to cup both breasts as the cloth dropped away. Trilloo looked externally like a Human, but this one had painted glitter in electric green on her areola, with a darker jade marking her nipples, both visible through the fingers slowly, lovingly kneading them.

Dirk found the vision arousing, shifting a little as he started to get hard. You could always learn a great deal about a woman by watching how she pleasured herself, especially when there were three of them.

The lone woman off to the side dropped her wrap now to reveal her pubic mound shaved into a green heart. She knelt at the edge of the stage and then rotated to turn her bottom to the audience slowly, allowing everyone to *ooh* and *ahh* as she flashed her sex at them.

Dirk thought he could detect a new scent in the air, but he wasn't sure if was the trio of dancers, something the bar was pumping into the air, or the beautiful green woman seated beside him, raptly watching the show as she sipped her wine.

Number Three flipped onto her back now, turned around to display everything with her legs in the air like a V. Number Two stripped completely naked as she watched and shimmied her way across the stage, kneeling down and straddling the other woman's face.

Dirk wondered idly if this situation qualified as masturbation or incest, when the woman on her back raised her head and began to lick her other self. Whatever it was, it appeared to be exactly what Number Two needed right now, because she began to writhe and buck out of tune to the music.

Number One joined them now on the floor now, still topless but wearing her wrap and kneeling beside them. Dirk had wondered if Number Two would move to sixty-nine, but that would have hidden too much from the crowd. Instead, Number One reached in a delicate hand and began to stroke Number Three's labia.

Up and down, penetrating just the slightest bit from time to time, and slowly increasing the pace as the music built and the smell of sex and musk grew with it. Fingers would disappear into a pussy that had to be soaking, from the way a spotlight began to glow. Dirk found his own hand twitching as he wanted to play the woman—women—like a well-tuned cello.

Number One moved up to her sister's clitoris now, circling it slowly, teasingly, and making the woman buck in rhythm to the music pulsing in the background. Number Two was grinding on Three's face and crying out like a recurring chorus.

The best part was that singular consciousness. All three of them tightened up and then orgasmed at once with a scream of pleasure, like a planetquake had hit, toppling the two into a pile of sweating, glistening blue flesh, moaning and jerking as they each grabbed some sensitive bit and worked that last drop of pleasure out of it.

Dirk was so hard now that he'd need to take some time before he could walk without discomfort. At least Tiffany hadn't slipped a hand under the table to stroke him during the show. Looking over, she was lightly rubbing herself through her dress instead.

The music had crescendoed at the same moment as the girls, and it faded now into quiet, letting the strings outside soothe everyone. Dirk looked over and found Tiffany's eyes almost glazed over with lust.

"If you found a male Trilloo, you could have every

hole stuffed at the same time, and then ride a triple orgasm as all three men filled you," he said quietly.

Her eyes turned his way, but she wasn't really seeing anything.

"Yeah," she said in a long sigh as she squirmed a little on the seat and withdrew the hand that had been resting in her lap.

He was hard from watching that masterful show. Tiffany was obviously aroused. Possibly, he should take her back to their room and bang the woman's brains the rest of the way out. Maybe just pull her into his lap right now and let her ride him until they both found some release from the tension that had risen.

They hadn't fucked on the flight here. Partly, that was him still being pissed at her bosses. Partly, he wanted to let it build with her.

Many fools thought foreplay was the last three minutes before penetration, without realizing that good foreplay started three minutes after she came, and lasted for hours, or days. Or months, in Tiffany's case. He hadn't seen her since…

Yes, best left unsaid. Unthought, even, lest it taint things going forward. Wasn't her fault, but she had apologized anyway, offering to make it up to him.

Not that she wouldn't have gotten something out of it.

They would fuck at some point. It would be loud, wet, messy, and mesmerizing. Probably make up for everything the Amaull Timocracy had dumped on him last time.

But not tonight.

Right now, he needed some food, another whiskey sour, and then to see a man about a horse.

DIRK HAD SENT Tiffany off to scout a few things and make contact with some of her folks who were apparently deep cover agents here in the casino or on the station. He didn't need to know who they were.

Instead, he had found his way to a table in an old-fashioned bar on a quieter concourse, the kind done up in wood paneling so dark as to be almost black, with copious use of brass and leather to give it a decidedly masculine feel.

Women weren't denied access, but the entire space was designed to make them feel subconsciously unwelcome. It attacked their femininity.

He shared the space with eighteen men and three women, none of them together. Each woman was dressed more like the men and carried themselves the same way. Androgynous and genderqueer, at least in dress. Sexuality or gender might be something entirely else.

Dirk shrugged. Plumbing didn't always agree with heart or desire, but them being in here was a statement that they most assuredly weren't looking for cock tonight. He also didn't need to seduce any of them for information, as far as he was aware.

That was fine, he had slipped a fifty cedi note to a porter along with a couple of questions that would get circulated. Eventually, they would find the right ears. On a station like this, it wouldn't even take all that long, as there was an entire world behind the pretty facade, back where all the employees were, hidden away from the beautiful people.

A man appeared at the door in full tuxedo, including Inverness-style opera cape, gloves, and even a walking stick. Dirk supposed that the only thing he was really missing was a top hat, but this entire station was functionally indoors and you never got any rain requiring it.

Ahlter Jenker. They weren't friends, but weren't enemies, last Dirk had checked.

Their eyes met and locked for a half-second before the man turned to the side and entered the cloakroom, emerging a few moments later without the accessories but still dressed at least to the eights, if not the nines.

He walked close and sat across from Dirk without an invitation.

They stared at each other for a long moment, and then a barmaid delivered a martini with three olives, withdrawing without a word or even a tip, so the man must be well known in here and have a running tab.

Dirk wasn't surprised. Ahlter Jenker was the highest of the high rollers. The kind of man who floor managers and casino owners knew on sight and treated like a veritable god because the money he routinely wagered.

Ahlter was medium height, but the cut of his tux and his lean shape always gave the impression of being taller. Dirk was always surprised to find that he was two inches taller than Ahlter when he ended up next to the man.

Rare gray eyes stared out from a dapper, sardonic face, framed by black hair brushed back from a widow's peak. He had a cruel mouth, thin and wide, but that didn't detract from the overall effect.

Friendly, but not your friend. It was a thin line, but Ahlter carried it off well.

"I would have thought that…" Ahlter began, but Dirk waved a casual hand.

"Water under the bridge," he replied obliquely, aware that certain statutes of limitations hadn't run out.

"But actually coming to *Jira*?" Ahlter continued, maybe still a bit amused.

"Doing a thing for a friend for a reason," Dirk smiled lazily. "You understand."

"I do," Ahlter nodded. "I was still rather surprised when your name came up."

"You own the joint yet?" Dirk shifted gears a little, gesturing to the room around them, and the whole station, with his glass.

He hadn't seen Ahlter in years. Anything might have happened.

"Too much work," the man grinned in reply, sipping at his martini and pulling out the first olive to munch on. "Easier to take a small percentage of ownership when they get that deep into me. I get better rates on things, and any money I do end up losing comes back, at least in part."

He turned serious now, leaning forward to make this a conversation between men. Like this bar was designed for, however hokey and sexist that might be. The galaxy was a vast place.

"What brings you here, Dirk?" Ahlter asked bluntly.

Dirk considered the man. They went back almost two decades, running and slumming in similar circles. Ahlter Jenkins had started out as a card sharp and conman, but somewhere along the way he'd taken a big-time player for what people called *fuck-you-money*, and retired from the game. Or just moved into a new con, depending on how you wanted to look at it.

"Tracking a rumor," Dirk said, watching the man's eyes. "Rayne Summers is going to come here, if she hasn't already."

"The Princess?" Ahlter gasped quietly. "What's she up to now?"

"Looking for something," Dirk said. "More likely someone. I don't have many of the details yet, but we don't any of us assume a woman like that is on the level."

"If she was crooked like me, I'd trust her more," Ahlter said sardonically. "Dirk Thruster here to thwart her again?"

"Too early in the con to know, Ahlter," he replied. "Might be nothing. Might be everything. Figured it would be worth calling on some old comrades and maybe finding a friendly face who'll be invited to those cocktail parties."

"You'll be on the invite list, as soon as anybody knows you're here, Dirk," Ahlter pointed out unnecessarily.

"True, but I'm the mark on this con," he smiled now. "She's got a lot of money and influence, and a need for something. Somebody is going make a little scratch on the side. Might as well be you as anyone."

"I don't need the money these days, Dirk," Ahlter laughed. "I had a rich auntie who died and left me everything in her will. I'm sure you've heard the story."

Dirk chuckled.

"Hey, if you've gotten too rusty to con the Princess, you could just come right out and say it, Ahlter," he fired back, watching the man's eyes.

They flared with indignation for an instant, before shifting to laughter.

"Touché, my friend," he chuckled now and speared his second olive. "But you could always just fuck the information you needed out of her. Or are the stories one hears true?"

"Depends on your source for the veracity," Dirk circled sidelong now with his words.

"Stunningly beautiful woman," Ahlter replied. "About as exciting in bed as fucking a dead shark."

"Oh, she's not that bad," Dirk said, before he paused and continued. "But there is a kernel of truth there."

"So you want me to long-con her with a magic box?" Ahlter smiled.

"As I said, someone's going to, once word gets out," Dirk returned the smile. "Might as well do a favor for a friend, instead of letting some punk kid hooligan have a go at her. Figure she'd just chew him up and toss him on the trash pile, if she didn't send him out an airlock."

Ahlter nodded.

"You're staying on the ship itself?" he asked.

"For now," Dirk replied. "At some point, someone will connect the dots and upgrade me to the Imperial Suite. When she gets here, there will be the obligatory expectation of staying on her ship so we can all have tea together or something."

"I see," Ahlter said. "And we don't know what she's after yet?"

"Information, my sources tell me," Dirk confided. "But I don't know any more than that, because I'm at the far end of the communications chain. You know how those get garbled."

"Indeed, I do," Ahlter replied, spearing the last olive and emptying his glass before he started to chew. "Sounds like fun, Dirk."

He rose and made his way to the cloakroom now, leaving Dirk to contemplate the room. One of the women in the corner was staring at him as if she wasn't sure who he was. The one he'd marked earlier by the way she'd been studying him out of the corner of her eye when he walked in. Dirk toasted her with his glass and leaned back to think.

The *Jira Sleeper Ship* was known galaxywide as a casino resort. It had been a colony ship a millennia ago, hauling fifty thousand Humans to Dr'Gonai in cryo-sleep. They'd left the shell in orbit afterwards and some investors had turned it into a casino. A destination event, drawing people in from all corners of the galaxy.

He could only speculate wildly on what the princess might think she was going to find here. Unless she was supposed to meet someone here who had her clue.

Penetrating the Forbidden Triangle. Possibly gaining access to hundreds of new worlds, or finding secret civilizations that had hidden themselves away. Exotic new technology? Something that would let her embrace her dreams of *Imperial Destiny*?

Texas was a wealthy-enough planet that King Zerik could indulge her with her own warship, and the Tantric Legion she had built. Wasn't like Rayne had enough firepower to threaten a populated planet, but she could make herself a nuisance.

A shadow interrupted his musing.

That one genderqueer woman from across the way wasn't across the way anymore. She'd risen, glass in hand, and stood next to him his table, nodding to the empty chair.

Dirk nodded back and she sat.

Her overall look went well with her open necked tuxedo shirt and jacket.

In fact, minus the tie she wasn't dressed all that differently from Ahlter, but Dirk hadn't done more than process her as being in the room. This place wasn't where you came to troll for dates. The men were usually presenting as strictly het and the women were presumed to be lesbians. At least that was the accepted norm. Zeros and Sevens on the Kinsey Scale, as it were. There were other bars catering to more exotic needs that fell in between.

Stydying her now, she was presenting as at least a Five in her look. But at the same time a Seven wouldn't be giving him that particular smile.

Call if a low Six. Generally lesbian, but occasionally willing to dabble. That smile said so right now.

Short hair, either frosted or naturally a gold so pale that it might be white in the right light. Butch cut, but only in that hers wasn't more than an inch long on the sides, and spiked on top into something of a rockabilly fauxhawk, while Dirk generally kept his swept back and onto a collar if he wore one.

Hazel eyes that seemed to dance back and forth between gold and green, depending on the light as he watched her watch him. Skin with a pale gold tan that didn't seem to have any freckles, but with modern chemistry, anything was possible.

Mature, if he could say that without being offensive. Probably straddling forty, like that Trilloo dancer had straddled her other self's face earlier. But it was a warm, friendly forty, rather than the kind where she'd been rode hard and put away wet too many times. The age was just starting to show in the neck and the back of the hand holding the glass, but that just suggested that she had enough experience in life to know what she was doing. What she wanted. And that maybe she wasn't afraid to ask for it. Possibly even cook you breakfast in the morning.

They shared a small smile.

"You look familiar, but I can't place you," she began in a throaty alto.

"I get that a lot," Dirk replied ambiguously. "Everyone seems to know a guy that looks just like me, back on their home planet."

"So that draws strangers into weird conversations?" she pressed.

"They aren't all weird," Dirk smiled easily now. "They just start out that way."

"And this just started weird?" the woman asked leadingly. "Before it goes somewhere else?

She was holding a highball glass that looked like it also contained whiskey, lemon sour mix, and ice, like his.

Dirk shrugged.

"Just two guys having a chat in a club," Dirk offered ambiguously.

"I'm not a guy," she said pointedly, even as her voice remained barely above a whisper.

Dirk gestured to the room with his free hand.

"In here you are," he said, staring more closely at her now.

"So if I wanted to be a woman, I'd need to take you somewhere else?" she teased.

"Do you even like boys?" Dirk asked quietly.

"Boys? Not at all," she said with a sharp, cruel laugh. "Men? That's a different matter. So few measure up to even be worth consideration."

Dirk sipped at his glass and studied the woman's body language. Hints of lust underneath and obvious desire. Intelligence in her eyes. Strength in her hands. Suggestions that she'd be willing to dip well down the scale, if he pressed his suit right now.

"Hard to find men on this station?" he asked, just to see where her mind wanted to go.

"Those other places are filled with little boys," she said. "They're hard, but have about as much technique as doing pushups. Most of them think the clitoris is a fairy tale, and that they have a magic penis that can induce vaginal orgasms every time. But that's because after a while a woman gets bored and fakes one just to make him get off her."

She paused and took a drink, eyeing him over the rim of her glass as she did.

"They don't know where to touch a woman," she continued.

"And I do?" he asked innocently, not suggesting anything but curiosity now.

"Your eyes do," she purred now. "They see me in this man's suit, but they aren't fooled. They imagine hips hidden by the cut of cloth and the fall of a jacket. Breasts that like to be kissed. Places to trace fingers and orgasms that never once involve penetration."

"I sound pretty impressive on paper," Dirk replied. "What if I can't live up to it?"

"You won't know until you try now, will you?" she pressed.

"And suppose I like boys?" he asked, just to watch the flare of lust in her eyes.

Just because a woman presented genderqueer didn't mean anything. She might be entirely het, and just enjoying the ability to have a drink in a place where nobody was likely to hit on her.

Safe space, as it were, rather than icky or dangerous.

"You wouldn't be here, either," she said dryly, tracing her tongue across her lips with just a quick bite that was gone so fast anyone else might have missed it. "None of these types can put up that good of a presentation."

"Ah, but I had to meet a man," he noted, nodding towards the door where Ahlter had left. "Do some business."

"And your business is done now?" she grinned with one side of her mouth.

"With him," Dirk returned the smile. "But I'm not sure what comes next. Or rather, where I might go."

He noted that she still hadn't introduced herself, nor asked his name. Just two strangers who'd run into each other on a train and chatting. However, given the circumstances, Dirk supposed that this might be as close to a perfect zipless fuck as one might arrange, assuming no ulterior motives from the woman.

"How far did you want to go?" she asked, again leading the conversation off safe ground.

"I'm just an innocent babe enjoying a whiskey sour," Dirk said, willing to test the bounds of her agency.

And ambition.

They were aboard the *Jira Sleeper Ship*, after all. The place where you went to do things that you didn't necessarily talk about when you returned to your homeworld. Certainly not one of those worlds where you might get prosecuted for sinning.

"But you might be led astray?" she asked now, still biting her lip.

"I'd have to have a destination in mind, in order to go astray," he pointed out. "Otherwise, we can't get lost. Just well-traveled."

"I see," she said, leaning forward now and putting her forearms on the table between them.

It had the effect—probably intended—of flaring out the lapels of her jacket to frame the line of where her nipples were pointed against the thin white linen underneath. Hot, dark spots that appeared to be in need.

Dirk wondered how sensitive they were to the kiss. Or if he should bring a cup of ice cubes to bed to have them handy.

"See?" she smiled. "Breasts distract you. You do like women."

"Never said I didn't," Dirk countered. "But show me a gay man who objects to them."

She smiled. Elbows still on the table, she reached up with the hand not holding the highball glass and deftly snicked a button open. The next one she would loosen formed a line with both of those nipples, but this showed him the valley of her cleavage, with both hills coming to points.

Dirk met her eyes now and locked on, daring her to open the shirt the rest of the way.

Something like reserve kicked in. She blushed.

That was one of the few reactions that could not be faked. And possibly the first honest emotion out of her since she sat down.

It wasn't that she was lying, as far as he could tell. She was putting on a show. A genderqueer one, at that. Presenting as something she probably wasn't, although he'd not had much of a glimpse at the woman underneath.

Dirk leaned forward now. Their hands weren't—quite—touching.

"What do you really want?" he asked in a sound barely above a whisper.

She hesitated for a moment, eyes flickering, but it was nerves, not lies.

"To find a dark corner and see if you kiss as well as I think you would," she finally murmured back

"But no more?" he asked, pushing on her boundaries now, rather than the other way around.

In a tango, he had just forced the pace. She shifted adroitly enough.

"I didn't say that," she replied, a little breathless.

"Oh?" Dirk smiled. "So if I pushed things a little further…?"

"I might not resist you," she said, again biting her lip, but he couldn't decide if it was a tell or a distraction.

"I see," Dirk said. He emptied his glass of the last

mouthful and set it down between them. "Then let's find out."

He rose suddenly. She reared back for a moment, caught herself, and finished her own drink, rising to stand beside him.

She was tall for a woman. Five foot ten, give or take, so he had about three inches on her.

Still androgynously slender, but that meant she looked to be made of hard-packed muscle, assuming she'd always been female.

He smiled and gestured for her to lead, still interested that she hadn't offered even a fake name at any point, nor asked his.

Zipless fuck, or set-up job. One could never be too sure, and he'd encountered both in his time.

Out into the corridor, he had to admit that the pants had been tailored to best effect on that bottom. Muscular and powerful. Broad in a sexy way.

She didn't have the sort of sway that Tiffany had been all about earlier, but Tiffany had been all in on distracting your eyes with sex, while this woman was declaring herself not interested in your penis, regardless of your opinion on the matter.

Out of the main corridor with all the crowds of tourists rushing about, she took him down a side hall, and then stopped at a door that seemed to be for staff, judging by the security control on the side.

The woman pulled an employee-style badge from the pocket of her jacket and waved it at the box. The door unlocked and she pulled it open.

Going down back hallways, is it? He wondered how far she might want to stretch that metaphor later.

Dirk was familiar with these sorts of places. Industrial and banal, because decoration was too expensive, even with the sorts of margins a successful casino ran.

I mean, what kind of idiot goes broke running a casino?

There was staff back here, mostly dressed in the black of waiters and waitresses, but a few in the colorful tunics of guides. Those meant to stand out.

She turned down another side corridor, and then another. He wasn't lost in the slightest, just interested in where she might be taking him.

The woman answered that by stopping at another closed door and peeking up at him from under hooded brows, wearing a naughty smile that promised everything and nothing.

The card came out again and they were inside.

Storage closet, near as he could tell. Shelves on three sides with what looked like staff uniforms. The lights were at about half, but she hadn't raised them when she came in.

Dirk made a note of the location, in case he ever needed to impersonate someone on duty.

She turned and backed herself into a corner, literally as well as metaphorically now.

"We're alone," she announced, as if he was going to be surprised by that. "Just how far did you want to go?"

"We seem to have reached the end of the line," Dirk offered, stopping about halfway between the door and the place where her body was within easy reach.

"Oh, this is just a quiet place where I could taste you," she said. "From there, we'll see how it goes. And where."

"Will we now?"

Dirk took that last step, sliding right up to the point where she might press her nipples against him if she took too deep a breath. He telegraphed slowly, watching her eyes for clues.

His right hand went down and simply rested on her left hip. Not pulling. Not gripping. Just resting.

She cocked her head up at him and smiled, so he put his left hand up, under her arm and around her, where it came to rest cupping a shoulder blade like a breast.

Her arms wrapped him, as well, one up around his neck and the other at his waist.

The first kiss was tentative, but got more powerful as they held it. Her mouth parted and he tasted her tongue with his.

Dirk gripped that hip now, thumb on the front of the bone where he could feel her move. She responded by pressing her breasts against his chest until he thought it might be painful. Her hand went up into his hair and caught just enough to tug, but not pull.

Dirk was semi-hard at this point, just from the fun of verbally dancing with the woman. Her heart was pounding rapidly against his ribs. He ground his cock against her groin.

Eventually, she broke the kiss and lowered her arm. Dirk wondered which path they be taking now.

Something hard poked him in the ribs as she leaned back, away from the kiss.

"That was everything I ever imagined it would be, Dirk," she said dreamily. "Everything the rumors suggest."

So, she knew his name.

He started to glance down, but she poked him harder, still holding his waist.

"Ah, ah, ah," she shook her head. "I've got a nervefire pistol pointed at you right now. Any sudden moves and I'll pull the trigger."

For a moment, he considered lashing out. He'd fallen for a trap baited with exotic fair, and it was going to get him in trouble. A set up from the get-go. A nervefire pistol would probably take him down if he did anything. Maybe he could put the woman down or even kill her, but he needed information.

Retribution could wait.

Dirk kept hold of the woman, hand on her hip and shoulder blade, his thigh still wedged into her groin like lovers. There was really no space to maneuver in here, and he wasn't sure which of his enemies she might represent.

Juno knew he had accumulated enough of them over the years.

"So now what?" he asked, wary of the situation and wondering where it would go.

If all else failed, he was still close enough to hammer her in the face with a headbutt. Good way to give someone a concussion, but for that pistol that would outline every nerve in his body in acid before he could recover.

"We're going to go upstairs and see someone, Dirk," she said, still close enough that he could smell the wintermint drop she'd chewed earlier. "Nothing terrible.

Just a few questions begging for answers. If you behave, I won't have to shoot you."

He disliked the way her eyes surged a little at the word *have*. Clearly, she was the type who might do it just for fun at some point. Dirk held his anger close and let his face remain neutral.

He nodded at her words, acknowledging her power over him. For now. Again, no place to maneuver. Or avoid getting shot.

"I'm going to let go with my left hand now," he said simply, waiting for her to nod. "And now my right. Stepping back slowly and carefully. Now what?"

She nodded and relaxed a little as space opened between them, as if she'd been expecting something rough in the clinch. It would be different kind of rough, had she held that pistol even a little wrong, and Dirk was certain she didn't know the right safe word for what he would have done at that point.

"Now, you'll turn away from me and walk to the door," she said in a much harder voice. Like a different woman. "In the hallway, you'll turn left and we're going to walk about thirty yards to a bank of elevators. I'll be behind you a few paces, but if I think you're about to do anything, I'm willing to just shoot you and call for someone to bring a wagon along so I can haul your unconscious body where it needs to go. I'd prefer not to have to make a scene, you understand."

"Perfectly," he nodded. "Opening the door and left to the elevator bank."

"Very good, Dirk," she cooed at him, that nervefire pistol never wavering.

The hallway outside was largely empty, but they were in a disused corridor. She'd planned that.

Dirk walked deliberately, placing each foot as he went and assuming she was far enough away that she could shoot him before he could escape, but not so far distant that he could dodge a bolt.

Nervefire pistols were twitchy beasts. They really only had an effective range of about twenty feet if you wanted to bring somebody down. But even a grazing blow would stagger him enough for the woman to finish him off.

Dirk had always said that he wanted to walk to his execution, whoever ended up with the task. Just not today.

So he walked. Precisely. Did not allow the rage in his belly to echo by stomping on the tiles under his feet.

The elevator bank was on his left in a vestibule. Four doors, two on each side of a compact room.

He entered and felt her behind him.

"Press the up button, Dirk," she said simply.

There was no music in this part of the facility. No color on the walls other than hard white. Speckled gray tiles that would hide scuffs.

Just the two of them.

Dirk pressed the button and turned.

She was closer now. Six feet away instead of the ten that would have been wise, but the space constrained her again. She compensated by holding her pistol close against her hip, where it was out of sight of somebody walking by, and hard for him to knock away.

He had exactly one chance, before he was trapped in that elevator, under the control of someone else.

She knew it too, from the way her pupils got small.

Dirk smiled at her breezily and turned to the corridor more or less behind her.

"That's it, Joe," he said in a conversational tone. "You can go ahead and arrest her now."

She spun, preparing to shoot whoever had snuck up on her.

Dirk drove hard off the balls of his feet and slammed into the woman, wrapping his larger hand around hers and pressing it against her stomach while he used his mass to bounce her off the wall behind her.

She might have been tall, but he still outweighed her by fifty pounds. And he was mad. Not desperate, yet, but close.

And, oh so very angry.

All the air rushed out of her lungs and she lost her grip on the pistol, squeezed between the immovable object of a station bulkhead and the irresistible force of Dirk's rage.

He stepped back, holding her pistol on her as she leaned back and tried to catch her breath.

Those hazel eyes turned golden when she was angry. He could testify to that later, if it were ever necessary.

"Now what?" she gasped weakly.

A ding filled the air around them and the door behind her suddenly opened, staggering her backwards into the lift she'd made him summon. She caught herself inside the small space, a trapped animal prepared for mortal combat.

Dirk smiled and shot her.

She collapsed with a small scream, really not much more than a squeak.

He reached in and pressed the top floor button, leaning out as the door closed between them.

"Hope it was worth it," he smiled at the impersonal barrier.

Dirk slipped the pistol into his pocket, along with her keycard that he'd grabbed when his body slammed her, then set off for the public spaces of the casino.

Someone would be able to tell him who she was.

Or at least who she worked for.

THE TANTRIC LEGION

TIFFANY HAD to remind herself that Dirk trusted her to handle her portion of this mission. That he hadn't just sent her off to get her out of his hair. She was a Senior Deputy of the Amaull Timocracy, undercover and intent on stopping that damnable Princess Rayne of Texas from whatever it was the rich bimbo thought she's do to take over the galaxy this time.

Still, in rankled. At the same time, it was necessary, as he'd pointed out. Dirk didn't need to know who her deep cover contacts on this ship were, any more than she needed to know who he was contacting from his extensive list of old friends and occasional lovers.

Maybe that was it. She'd spent most of the flight to Dr'Gonai teasing the man, but they hadn't fucked. It would have taken some of the edges off her tartness. They were both aware of that, so maybe he intended her to be wound a little tighter than normal.

After all, they were now aboard the *Jira Sleeper Ship,*

home of some of the greatest carnal pleasures civilized beings could consensually inflict on one another. Anything was possible, if you had time, money, and patience.

Tiffany would have liked to seek out one of the Shibari experts aboard, but now was most definitely not the time or place to be bound and helpless. Not while they were seeking unknown enemies hiding in the shadows.

Instead, she'd taken something that would cause her green-dyed skin to turn almost indigo for ten hours or so. Her long hair was up now in a braid that had been tripled under to make it seem much shorter. She wore a white silk bandeau sized for a woman with a smaller chest, such that she threatened to spill out of it every time she breathed too deeply. And her nipples remained starkly outlined.

Tiffany's shoes were hardly more than ballet slippers, and she wore nothing more but a pair of boyshorts in black and a leather belt containing several closed pockets with anything she thought she might need.

Most of her purpleness was visible, and the smile on her face suggested that you could see the rest if you asked nicely. Tiffany didn't need cock tonight, but after all the teasing and such with Dirk and Rico getting here, she didn't think she'd be able to resist all that much, if the right one came along on this mission. Or the right pussy.

She slipped into the dance club quickly, feeling the intense pulse of the music hit her in a sonic wave. Space stations never slept, and *Jira* was even worse about that. The party might ebb and flow in here, but they just traded off bartenders and bouncers and regularly hauled people out who had passed out from dancing or drink.

Right now the space was at a lower ebb, so maybe

she'd timed it right. Her contact had suggested the time as well as the place, so presumably that woman knew the bionetic rhythms.

Tiffany made her way across what turned out to be the second floor of the club, a mezzanine with transparent floors and a railing around open gaps to lean on while watching the dancers below. The outer walls of the mezzanine were a continuous series of bars, broken up by lots of restrooms, with dozens of bartenders on duty to service the five hundred or so folks she could see on both levels.

The music was an audio assault in here. The drinks were salted and salty snacks were free for the taking. Anything to get you to spend more money at the bar because you were hot and thirsty.

Looking around, Tiffany was only barely on the provocative side of center with her dress, and then only because her breasts were covered. Most Human planets still had some public nudity issues, but that was a cultural thing. Here, as long as nobody was actually fucking on the dance floor, the bouncers probably wouldn't bother you. They only did then because someone might get hurt, trying something like that surrounded by others trying to dance. That and shoes to protect your feet seemed to be the only rules.

She made her way to an edge and got a watered down drink. That was fine. Cheap and easy. She dropped a small pill in and watched it dissolve. She was safe against poisoning or being roofied unless it turned bright pink.

Even here, a girl had to watch her back against predators. They stalked the tourists who might not necessarily be missed, and certainly wouldn't want to remain around after their vacation ended to testify at a trial about what someone might have done to them.

All the seats were downstairs, in levels surrounding the dance floor like an inverted ziggurat. Some folks came to places like this just so they could wear a miniskirt with nothing under it and stand only feet above the highest booths below, while others took those booths for the show overhead.

All manner of peep shows became available when there was a thick piece of plexiglass between the two of you. Especially if the two players could meet up later.

Tiffany found a spot upstairs and leaned against the rail, ass stuck out like she was inviting a caress, but that was still a matter of convention. It was always rude to touch uninvited, especially in places like this, and the bouncers were big, mean-looking folks with no sense of humor.

Below, the first song ended and a new one started. There were stages in two corners above the dance floor and a new sex show started up as well, MFM in one corner and FMF in the other, both sets Human, as far as she could tell. The players were largely ignoring the music and focusing on themselves instead.

In the closer show she watched, the woman had stretched out on her back, where she could just wrap her mouth around one man's cock as he was on hands and knees over her. Then the other man approached the first man and mounted him, long, slow strokes that the woman matched with her mouth.

Tiffany had never had the sort of long-term mission

where she'd needed to grow a penis, so she could only imagine the pleasure of having a cock that someone could suck on while someone else was penetrating her ass. And stretching it. The man at the rear had a wide cock, though it hadn't looked that long.

The man in the middle had a longer, skinnier cock, but the woman was just working the glans and frenulum with her mouth, rather than trying to fit the entire thing in her mouth and presumably down her throat.

Tiffany imagined herself laying there, with Dirk straddling her. Or maybe Rico in her mouth and Dirk taking him. She'd never done both of them at once, but knew that both men were fairly open-minded about their sexuality.

As Dirk had said more than once, "Does it really matter who makes you cum?"

Tiffany sipped on her drink, letting the ice cool her down before she completely overheated and soaked through her boyshorts.

In the other corner, the one man was on his back, with one woman riding his cock and the other astride his face. The women kissed hotly to complete the triangle, hands groping every which way, pulling, probing, penetrating, teasing.

Tiffany shifted around enough to rest her nipples on the cold, metal rail, letting that jolt her nerves as she watched the two trios pleasure each other. In the booths below her, more than one couple or small orgy was also putting on a show, but those tended to be awkward in the tight confines and hard to watch unless you were directly overhead.

Similarly, Tiffany had her legs spread just far enough apart that one could follow her legs from ankles to heaven while watching from below. Or behind, but that space was empty.

A woman appeared on her right. Stepped close enough to share the railing companionably, but not violating her personal space.

Not yet.

Tiffany wondered just what kinds of violations she might need later, with all the sexual energy going on around her right now.

The woman glanced over and flashed a quick hand sign. Tiffany was a bit surprised, but she'd never met this agent in person, only communicated via textcomm.

Tiffany returned the counter and the woman slipped a little closer, until their elbows and hips touched.

Ardel was tall. Six foot four or more, but she was proportioned more like a man, so her legs were about the same length as Tiffany's. Lean, almost to the point of starvation, but her arms didn't have any of the signs of deprivation, being smooth and muscular. Tiffany wondered if she had the metabolism of a hummingbird.

Capri pants to mid-calf accentuated her impossibly-long shape, as did a shirt that was skin-tight of the gray thinnest jersey. Small breasts pressed out. Almost no hips at all. Fingers that almost reminded Tiffany of tentacles, so long and thin.

Tiffany wondered how deep one might slip inside her. Not as good as a cock, but far more nimble to find all the spots needing touch.

She leaned close enough to Ardel to speak in her ear

over the pounding music.

"Can we actually talk here?" she asked, pressing a full breast against she woman's arm as she did.

Ardel didn't object to the touch. Leaned into a little, even.

She shifted around to put her lips against Tiffany's ear.

"It's actually a little quieter below," she said moistly, a tongue darting out to trace a circle on Tiffany's ear that seemed to echo in her groin, as though one of those long tentacles was circling her clitoris right now.

Tiffany turned and just kissed the woman, both of them awkwardly leaned forward. Ardel returned it with a hunger that seemed to match Tiffany's ardor.

Before things got out of hand, Tiffany leaned out of the kiss and watched the woman's eyes open, pupils shrinking back down.

"This way," Ardel said, taking her hand and leading Tiffany to a set of stairs nearby.

Below, it was less painfully loud. Tiffany assumed several sonic baffles were projecting at various strengths, until it was almost as quiet as a subway, clear up at the top. But those were also the most crowded booths, so Ardel led her to a booth about midway back, slipping into the empty space and flipping on a personal baffle to keep sound from escaping.

Tiffany didn't trust such things, as it would be too easy to plant listening devices inside and then filter through them for things you could blackmail someone over. As Ardel slid into the booth, Tiffany reached into one of the pockets on her belt and pushed a button to activate a white-noise jammer. The air filled with a harsh buzzing that drifted up and down like a flight of angry hornets circling.

The booth was squared off, where six could sit comfortably around the table top. Next to the sonic shroud, there were other buttons, where you could place orders for a waitress to deliver, or summon help if someone got overly enthusiastic. Tiffany ignored those and watched as Ardel stretched out flat on her back with a long leg up, bent at the knee in invitation.

Tiffany climbed atop the woman and found a comfortable spot to press her chest into the other woman's, kissing her again and trying not to grind too hard on her. It had been a long week, and she was horny, but the mission still came first.

Ardel seemed to understand, and concentrated on necking and heavy petting for a bit. That made it worse, but Tiffany would need a shower later anyway, just from the smells of tobacco and perfume. There was no reason it couldn't be a cold one.

"Archer," Ardel whispered at one point, when Tiffany had gone to work on her neck and ear.

"Expire," Tiffany countered.

"Oblivion."

"Colossus."

Ardel relaxed and started to grind herself against Tiffany now, confident that the woman really was who she said she was. Always a risk when meeting an agent you didn't know on sight.

"What do you need to know, Deputy?" Ardel gasped a little as Tiffany lifted her shirt and began sucking on a sensitive nipple.

They were tiny breasts. Hardly more than a nipple emerging from her pectoral muscles, but someone had once explained that they contained the same number of skin nerves as gigantic breasts, which made them exquisitely reactive to the touch. Tiffany's free hand explored the other one with a thumb, while her fingers traced ribs up and down.

Ardel seemed to be having a hard time breathing.

"Princess Rayne of Texas is supposedly in route, looking for someone or something," Tiffany explained to the nipple in question before putting it back in her mouth and feeling it harden even more.

Ardel squirmed, grinding herself against Tiffany's hip and stammering as she spoke.

"There have been rumors," Ardel managed to say, twitching verbally as well as physically. "They even suggest that the Tantric Legion might be here already."

Tiffany stopped sucking and nibbling so suddenly that Ardel whimpered and unconsciously pressed her breast forward. Tiffany gave it a quick kiss and then slid up to where they were face to face. She began kissing the woman lightly, letting some of the mad passion drain away.

If Rayne was already here, this might all be some sort of trap. She had to find out the truth.

Underneath her, Ardel was suffering an emotional letdown, for which Tiffany was sorry.

"We must find out if *The Libertine* is here, or the Tantric Legion," Tiffany whispered to the woman between kisses. "What do you need to do? Who do we need to talk to?"

Ardel shifted around to free a hand that peeled

Tiffany's bandeau up and out of the way now, freeing a breast for her to begin tweaking.

Overhead, Tiffany supposed that people would be enjoying the show. What other purpose did these booths serve except for voyeurs and exhibitionists to safety interact?

Ardel turned Tiffany on her side now and slid that incredibly long body down to where the taller could begin kissing an aching nipple, pausing to murmur sweet nothings of trade craft.

"We would need Flight Control if her ship is here," Ardel said, breathing cool air on a hot, wet nipple.

Tiffany bent down to kiss the woman's short, brown hair, and then run her fingers through it, gripping a little with each pass as Ardel hummed.

"What if she snuck in without the ship and only brought a small force of troops with her?" Tiffany asked with a gasp of her own as a warm mouth closed on her breast and a hand found the wetness in her boyshorts and slowly began to manipulate it.

"I can put out the word to my network to look more closely," Ardel said in between nips and kisses. "If the Tantric Legion is here, they probably won't keep a low profile. Those women stand out, even in disguise."

Tiffany agreed. She wanted to get lost in the tall woman's ministrations, but time might be critical, especially if Rayne had somehow gotten ahead of them.

She pulled Ardel up until they were face to face and kissed her longingly.

"While I'd love to put on a show for everyone here," she interrupted the physical action, "the mission is more important, so we need to look like we're going to go get private room somewhere instead as we leave. I need to alert my people and you need to talk to yours."

Ardel's face fell into sadness. She craned that long neck down for one last kiss and then pulled the bandeau back in place, not that it hid much with both diamond-hard nipples still outlined in the cloth.

Sliding backwards, she reached down and pulled Tiffany upright, pressing their bodies flat against each other and stealing one more kiss that had Tiffany reconsidering how soon she needed to move.

But this was the Princess. If she was here and being quiet, it was possible the woman had finally started to listen to her field commander. Jock Manhammer was good at what he did, and might have placed the galaxy at her feet, but she never seemed to take his advice, or seen how much the man was desperately in love with her.

From what stories circulated, the man had to settle for occasional pity fucks as the Princess pined after men like Dirk. Stupid, because he really did have a hammer. Tiffany had seen pictures of it and imagined it stretching her out.

Maybe she'd need to seduce the Manhammer on this mission.

She kissed Ardel one more time and took her hand like lesbian lovers headed out.

Things were getting complicated around here.

TIFFANY HAD LEFT a brief message for Dirk, and sent a more detailed update to Rico, a Dirk's pilot was currently hiding down on the planet for now. She sat in a quiet restaurant booth now, sipping hot tea as she checked a fresh message from Ardel.

Possible Tantric Legion sighting, it said, giving a location of a club in one of the quieter corners of the vessel. That address made sense if the Princess was trying to hide that she was really here.

Would that mean the situation was bigger than anybody had expected? Or had Rayne finally started to learn subtlety? Finally, was it all a trap, leaked to her people knowing they would most likely bring in Dirk?

She needed to explore before that, just to find out what kind of ground they might be fighting on later. That, however, brought its own problems.

The Tantric Legion was comprised exclusively of females. There were a few technical specialists and officers that were males, like Jock Manhammer, but everyone could pass for Human.

Tiffany was Human, under all this camouflage, but if she stripped it off and returned to her normal self, someone might recognize her. The Legion was huge, and constantly recruiting as women retired or got arrested for various things, but Tiffany'd been enough of a thorn in Rayne's side over the last few years that her picture was probably used as a target for weapon's training.

So, she couldn't necessarily penetrate the organization. At least not without some planning, and that required scouting.

At the same time, her indigo would last for another six hours or so. That was probably long enough for a quick scout. If she went longer, it wouldn't necessarily mean someone woke up to coyote ugly, but it also probably wouldn't be the first time the person they woke up next to looked nothing like the one they'd taken to bed.

Tiffany paid and grabbed her gear bag. Into the restroom, she swapped out the dancing clothes for something a little more touristy. Capri pants like Ardel had worn earlier, royal blue, and a black pullover shirt with long sleeves. She even went so far as to wear a brassiere, just because a lot of worlds still believed in torturing women with fashion.

Her hair was up, but she let it down and tied it in four places so that it was more like a leash the right woman might pull. If they managed to get lucky.

After all, you didn't have to be a lesbian to join the Tantric Legion. They'd train you. The lack of men around encouraged the women to get creative, but that would make Tiffany a new flavor for someone to try.

Ardel had left her wet and disappointed earlier, maybe she'd be able to get lucky physically, as well as with her mission.

Tiffany exited the club and made her way to one of the transport cars that ran back and forth on the various levels like a tiny subway system. The station was always crowded, and the platform was full when she arrived.

When Tiffany boarded the next car, she found herself pressed up against a middle-aged couple, Humans at least by appearance, with the husband giving the impression of a banker on vacation and the wife being the sturdy, staid homemaker trapped in a dead-end existence of knitting clubs and grandchildren.

Except that the wife was quietly staring at her as

Tiffany tried not to press up against them when the car went around a curve. That was when the woman delicately licked her lips and leaned forward, into Tiffany's arm.

Tiffany was so surprised that she didn't move, letting the woman press forward, rather than withdrawing. A hand in the closely-packed bodies found hers and squeezed it before moving it onto the woman's bottom and patting.

Their eyes were suddenly locked, and the woman smiled discreetly, even as her husband seemed oblivious, reading a tourist map or something. Tiffany caressed the muscle, tracing down to the back of the woman's thigh and then right up the center of her ass.

She saw the woman's eyes roll backwards a little and her eyelids fluttered, so Tiffany squeezed a little gasp out of the woman, her mouth opening up in a tiny O of surprise.

The woman's hand reached out and rested on Tiffany's hip now, fingers curling around the back and little and pulling forward, until Tiffany's groin was pressed against the shorter woman's hip bone. The jostling of the crowd as the car moved hid everything, but the woman's eyes spoke volumes of desire for a touch that had apparently been missing.

Tiffany gripped the housewife's ass tighter now and let the woman rub herself against Tiffany's thigh. She raised a hand, hidden in the crowd of bodies, and took the woman's breast in her palm, watching those eyes open wide for a moment before she sagged a little.

Neither of them speak, but the woman mouthed *Please* at Tiffany, so Tiffany lightly pinched the hardening nipple, wondering if the woman might faint from the way her breath caught and her skin flushed.

They rode like that for nearly a minute, a stranger's breast in her hand and the woman grinding on her leg, before the car entered the next station and the husband perked up.

"We've arrived, dear," he announced quietly, glancing at his wife apparently still oblivious to what had been happening just behind him.

"Coming," the woman said in a fluttery voice, making Tiffany wonder if she really was.

Their eyes locked once more and the woman mouthed *Thank you* before she slid away and Tiffany let her hands fall to her side.

Strangers on a train. She'd done weirder things. Maybe Ardel had gotten her so worked up that she'd been putting out the right musk.

Tiffany took a deep breath as the car got into motion again. There were far fewer riders now, so she wasn't bumping into people on curves. Hopefully, nobody could smell her, as aroused as she was right now.

Two stops later, she had reached the end of the line, so to speak. The car emptied as this was the last stop at the north end of the ship.

Tiffany emerged into a corridor and took an escalator up two levels. The crowds were thin here, and seemed to be comprised more of locals, rather than tourists. This area had the feeling of people who actually lived on the station as employees, all those various service workers in the front or back of the many casinos, hotels, restaurants, and brothels.

Everything was quieter here. Money lived elsewhere, and these folks wanted bland walls and floors, everything a soothing color. No music played over the sound of air systems pumping. Even the floor had been treated so that her footsteps were deadened.

Stopping to sniff, Tiffany couldn't detect any foreign scents in the air. Perhaps they were that close to the life support systems here that the air was still pure?

Interesting thought. Why would Rayne want to hide here?

Except that it was the sort of place nobody would be looking for her.

Tiffany McGee wasn't sure the universe was safe if the Princess was finally learning guile. That portended a change for the worse for everyone else, so she needed to get to the bottom of things.

She located her target destination and entered, a joint that felt more like a neighborhood bar than anything. Booths on the left, bar on the right, tables in the middle. Greasy food, freshly cooked, assaulted her nostrils as she entered, reminding Tiffany that she hadn't eaten in hours, and the chemicals she had taken were using up reserves.

"Wherever," the gruff bartender yelled at her, so Tiffany moved to a table towards the front.

The booths were about half empty, but she wanted more privacy, and they were too close together. Similarly, the bar itself seemed populated by true locals. Folks who lived within a three minute walk of the front door.

Depending on how you wanted to quantify it, the station's current time was more or less the middle of the night, based on the planet below them. They weren't geosynched, but tended to use that clock, so it was a few hours until dawn.

The downtime, when most people had gone home. Or, in this case, stopped here for food before sleeping after their shift. Not everyone in here was wearing some sort of work uniform, but more than half were as she looked around.

She didn't stand out, but didn't fit in, either.

A guy staggered out of the back with a menu in hand and a glass of water that he put down. Then immediately picked both back up, pulled a rag from a back pocket, and swiped the table once, which mostly just seemed to move the grease around, rather than cleaning it.

Tiffany smiled at him with her eyes, her mouth, and her chest.

"Coffee, please?" she asked.

He nodded, a little dumbfounded, and wandered off to the bar.

Bar food plus. That was a good way to classify the menu. Things you could either nuke in the microwave straight from the freezer, or fry up on an open grill in a hurry.

Nothing exotic or complicated. These folks had to deal with that at work. This was comfort food.

Eyes peeked at her from various corners as she appeared to concentrate on her menu. Indigo skin. Long, black hair. Nearly-perfect bones in her face. Nice tits. Even Dirk had complemented them.

Tiffany tried to project an air of faint innocence in the way she sat. Maybe the girl who ran away from home to live in Dr'Gonai, where she'd wallow in sin and then maybe be discovered and turned into a star.

Too many young people fell for the glitz and got swallowed whole by the machine, but they were technically adults, so she wasn't responsible for saving them.

As long as they were adults. Anything else and she'd be the one kicking in the door with a plasma bolter in hand. Or a splatterstik if she wanted prisoners to hang personally after they were found guilty.

But nobody was going to look at thirty-two-years-old Tiffany McGee and mistake her for a lost child. Maybe she was a girlfriend who had just arrived. Or a new worker just moving into the area.

Innocence, but not *that kind*.

Two booths in the back of the bar seemed interesting. Five people in one, six in the other. All female. All of a rough age and shape, from what she could see. Paying attention, but more in a militarily-alert way than just ogling the new girl.

Assuming Tiffany wasn't making things up to fill in the story in her head.

Barback Guy swaggered over with a mug of coffee and didn't spill too much setting it down.

"What'll ya have?" he asked with a cheesy, almost-winning smile that probably worked to disarm a lot of girls. Although looking closer at the man he seemed to be more of a threat to the boys.

"Cheeseburger," she replied. "Cooked just past bloody. Can you throw some gravy on the fries and poutine them?"

"Uh, maybe?" he replied, a little confused now. "Lemme ask Dak."

She saw him off and noted that most of the locals had gone back to ignoring her now. None of their business, and she should stay out of theirs sort of thing.

Which made the group in the corner stand out all the more. Tiffany sipped her coffee and played a role just past ingénue but not all the way down to cynical grump. A few rough edges that the right tongue might smooth over if you had the patience to try.

It had actually helped, that random encounter with the middle-aged banker's wife, or whoever the woman had been. Tiffany had needs right now. Feminine needs, especially after she'd also gotten so aroused earlier with the sex show at the club where she'd first met Ardel. A woman going down on her, with all the polite tenderness of her feminine side, rather than a cock, or even a butch, would be perfect about now.

A few delicate kisses in the right places would probably make her cum her brains out before she was even undressed.

Tiffany tried to bottle that up and waft it over the entire bar like a musky scent, just to see who bit. Or kissed. She sipped her coffee and glanced occasionally at the mob of women.

They weren't being rowdy. If anything, a little too quiet, like they were under strict orders to behave in public. But again, she might be reading things into the situation.

Hushed whispers and nudges over there drew her eye,

but nobody did more than make eye contact before quickly breaking it.

Tiffany grew a little more audacious now, staring outright. The four she could see easily on the outer edges were all of a particular look. Mid-twenties. Athletic. Female. Hair and skin color ranged across the spectrum, but nobody had any even long enough to touch a collar. A few had buzzed it to nothing on the side and little more on top.

Tiffany usually associated those haircuts with soldiers, since you had to keep it under a helmet all the time. The same with the bodies, as they were none of them even a little pudgy, which was usually unheard of in a group of a dozen women.

Unless they had a reason. Or a specific job.

A bottle blond with mahogany skin, seated on the outside of the back booth, facing Tiffany, had the best view and showed off the most. Pretty, but not gorgeous. Above average in many ways. A little more muscular, or perhaps just more compact. She gave the impression of five foot one, but more like someone had taken a woman of average height and squished her down a little, rather than scaling her to ninety percent.

The blond was eyeing Tiffany. From the looks and whispers going back and forth, there might be bets going on about how hard it might be for the woman to seduce the stranger. Given Tiffany's mission and the circumstances, that wouldn't be too hard, but she was still going to make the woman work for it.

Gift horses, and all that.

Barback Guy delivered her food now. Dak had

apparently known what poutine was, because he/she had managed a pretty good effect. Tiffany sliced the burger in half and watched it bleed on her plate.

"All good?" he asked.

"Just right," Tiffany smiled up at him.

He left and she dug in, even more famished just from the smell.

About halfway through the meal, the blond made her move. She hopped up and went to the restroom, and then took a long detour on the way back, approaching Tiffany slowly and with a hopeful smile on her face.

Tiffany gestured to the other chair as she crammed a bite of burger into her mouth, careful not to end up wearing any of the sauce. She'd need to find Dak's recipe. Or come back here more. It was amazing.

Blond slid into the chair with a grin, turning to smile back at all her friends before looking at Tiffany again.

"You don't look like a local," the woman began hesitantly.

Tiffany swallowed and smiled at her.

"Not my first trip to Dr'Gonai," she replied. "Staying elsewhere, but the food here is worth the trip."

And it was. She used a fork to grab fries, rather than wear gravy on her hands.

Unless she wanted to convince the blond to lick everything clean afterwards…

"So my friends were gonna head back to barracks in a bit and maybe have a little party," the blond continued. "I'm Wendra, by the way."

"Gan," Tiffany introduced herself with a pleasant lie. "Not sure I'm up to taking on all your friends."

Wendra blushed. Hard and bright red, even as dark as her skin normally appeared. Cute, too.

"Oh, not that," she stammered. "I was wondering if maybe we could find a quiet corner or something while they go get loud. Just you and me."

"You like girls, Wendra?" Tiffany purred at her, grabbing her burger for the last two bites.

She needed to be ready to move, one way or the other, and it would be a pity to leave something this juicy and perfect behind on the plate.

"Prefer them," the blond said, getting more onto stable ground. "Boys never really did it for me."

"I understand the feeling," Tiffany agreed.

Dirk, Rico, and a few others notwithstanding, a cock was just a cock, and most men really didn't understand how to use one correctly, which was a shame.

"Someplace quiet?" Tiffany asked around the last bite as she chewed quickly. "You said barracks earlier. That sounds loud and open and maybe like we'd have an audience."

"Oh, that's just a figure of speech," Wendra stammered some more. "Boss has us all in a private wing. Single rooms not much bigger than coffins."

"Boss?" Tiffany turned innocent. "He going to mind you recruiting while you're here?"

Buzzwords. Little things in speech that trigger unconscious responses. Tiffany had put the emphasis on *He*, but Wendra had spiked on *recruiting*.

"Oh, she, not he," she said.

"She?" Tiffany let confusion show on her face. Like a

female boss was a weird thing, rather than absolutely normal.

Some worlds were still a little backwards that way.

Wendra blushed again.

"Yeah," she agreed. "Not supposed to say much. Kinda a secret."

"And you bringing a date home won't get you in trouble?" Tiffany teased.

"Only if it was a guy," Wendra brightened up. "I'd catch all kinds of hell from the girls if I needed a cock that wasn't fake."

Tiffany noted that all of her burger was gone, along with most of her fries. She munched and studied the intruder, as if trying to work up the nerve to actually go home with a total stranger in a bar, instead of plotting communications check-ins and escape routes in her mind.

"Well, I was supposed to meet some friends later," Tiffany hedged. "But not for a couple of hours. Lemme send her a note and let her know I'm making a side stop first. Your place got a shower I could use?"

"Nope, we're in a dorm kind of thing there," Wendra said.

"That's fine, I can shower when I get to her place then," Tiffany nodded.

She reached into a pocket to pull out cash as well as her handcomm. Quickly, she typed a coded message to Ardel with instructions that meant she was to reach out to Dirk in six hours if no subsequent message had arrived.

Ardel responded in a matching code almost immediately, using a frowning face and saying that "they'd hook up later then."

Tiffany left cash and a tip on the table as she stood.

"Shall we?" she looked down on the shorter woman as she stood up.

Tiffany had a whole head on the woman. Something like ten inches, so almost the opposite of what it would be like with Ardel. It would be interesting to put two women with that great of a height difference together, but Tiffany remembered a man who had once told her that every woman is four foot ten when you get her horizontal.

He'd understood what that meant and how to use it.

Wendra took her hand a little shyly as they exited, the woman blushing fiercely as her comrades hooted and cat-called behind them.

"Ignore the girls," Wendra said as they got into the corridor. "They're just jealous."

Tiffany stopped her for a quick kiss, just to break the ice and so it wouldn't be as awkward later. They broke and headed towards a side corridor, up another level, and into a private wing that required a passcard to access. Tiffany was pretty sure she could hack the system, but it would be noisy to do.

The space beyond was much more expensive looking. Carpet now, instead of painted metal. Wall hangings and half-paneling. The doors were relatively close together, but Tiffany was familiar with these sorts of places. You had a bunk barely wide enough for two bodies, possibly stacked two tall. Drawers underneath for clothes. A chair in the corner. Maybe seven feet wide and perhaps ten deep, almost like being on a military starship, where space was at a premium.

Wendra stopped at one and fumbled with her card as

Tiffany came up behind her and wrapped her arms around the woman's midsection in a hug that pressed her breasts against Wendra's neck. Distracting. Promising. *Offering.*

It took the shorter woman a moment to get the door to slide open, and then they were inside. Compact, just as Tiffany had expected. Empty, so not any sort of ambush, which was always a risk.

Wendra turned and Tiffany stepped into her, sharing a long, slow kiss. Tiffany was pleased but not surprised to find that the woman was all muscle as she explored the smaller woman's back and bottom. Assuming that Wendra was Tantric Legion that would fit, as those women were constantly training.

Hands began to roam, exploring bodies and then sliding under shirts to test flesh. Shoes got kicked randomly into a corner. It took Wendra a few tries to locate the hook holding Tiffany's brassiere in place, but that was because it was in front. Both hands had to come up and cup her breasts to get a good grip and then they rather exploded it open when the hook unlatched.

Tiffany slithered out of her shirt and let the bra fall as well before reaching out and starting to strip Wendra.

The shorter woman's breasts were broad and flat, hanging down some and stiffly at attention as Tiffany bent down to kiss each of them. She'd be back for more soon.

"Pants?" Wendra asked.

Tiffany smiled and pushed her backwards to the edge of the bed.

"Later," she said as she pressed the woman onto her back and then climbed into the bunk and pressed her chest against Wendra's for another slow kiss.

She needed the release, but also needed to bring the other woman along.

Nobody ever said that espionage and law enforcement couldn't be fun.

Tiffany ended up on her back at one point, with Wendra's weight between her legs and the woman going back and forth on her nipples, kissing and tugging as Tiffany got wetter and wetter. A little friction right now and she might just cum the first time before she even got her pants off.

Wendra seemed to sense that, as she slowed down and began kissing in other places, just tracing her tongue here and there while fingertips left acid marks of fire on Tiffany's nerves.

Finally, Tiffany grabbed Wendra by the hair to pull her up.

"I need to cum, right now," she demanded.

Wendra smiled and kissed her.

Pants vanished next, piled on other clothing. Tiffany never had tan lines in her line of work. Right now, she had turned everything purple, with black hair everywhere.

Wendra, however, did have patterns. Pale skin where she wore something like a sports bra to contain her chest while outdoors. Tanned, flat stomach. White where she wore shorts in the sun and boots with socks.

The bed was barely long enough for Wendra to go down on her, so Tiffany slid all the way up and diagonal. Later, she'd sixty-nine the woman. There was space for it, but right now her pussy was on fire and she needed someone to take care of it.

Wendra ought to be able to smell her need. Tiffany

could. And Wendra lapped with a long, delicate tongue as Tiffany threatened to drown her.

Tiffany was already so close that she began to shake immediately. Wendra simply reached up with both hands onto her hip bones to hold her down while she tongue-fucked Tiffany.

Too much. Too soon.

Or maybe it had been too long.

Tiffany came immediately, but Wendra didn't back off. Didn't slack. She only moved up enough to wrap her lips around Tiffany's clit and suck lightly as the first orgasm exploded with a scream that might be audible in the hallway through the closed door and then a second one came right behind it.

With what little brain was left, Tiffany felt a moment of pity for the men that only got one orgasm before they were done. She hit her third and then Wendra dropped back down and took both sensitive labia into her mouth.

Fourth that was bigger than the second. Fifth that was more of an aftershock. Sixth nearly made her pass out, so Tiffany grabbed at Wendra's hair and pulled her up and away.

Everything was so hypersensitive right now that just breathing on her pussy might hurt. Wendra seemed to understand. She smiled like a cat with a canary and slipped up to lay next to Tiffany as more aftershocks rippled through her body.

Damn, I really needed that.

Tiffany wondered if there was any truth to the legends of secret lessons in the tantric arts that Rayne's troops learned. If so, she might have to talk her bosses into letting her go deep cover in the organization sometime, just for more of *those*.

The room was too bright. And spinning.

Wendra kissed her on the tip of the nose.

"When I can think again, I'll do that to you," Tiffany whispered.

"Deal," Wendra grinned and just laid there.

Didn't take as long as Tiffany expected to recover, but it also hadn't been someone like Dirk spending an hour on her pussy first, working her up and down the scale before the culmination. That might have taken two minutes. Not quite a new record, but Tiffany knew she'd needed the release.

She opened her eyes and mouth and pounced on Wendra's lips, tasting her tongue and her on juices. Lovely. She was tart right now. Musky.

"So what can I do to you?" Tiffany asked slyly, one hand drifting down the smaller woman's chest and past her belly button until it encountered cloth she slid under.

Wendra was wet. Clean shaven, too, or possibly waxed. Maybe they were taking chemicals now to keep pubic hair at bay while not bothering the rest.

Wendra pressed against her exploring fingers and clenched up as Tiffany traced both directions on her sensitive labia.

"I really want some cock," the woman said. "But what you're doing it fine."

"Do you have one lying around?" Tiffany asked, slipping two fingers up inside the woman now and curled them upwards to tap lightly on her g-spot.

Wendra nearly levitated off the bed with a gasp.

"Yeah," she managed to wheeze.

"Where?" Tiffany asked.

"Footlocker, but I gotta open it," Wendra whispered.

Tiffany withdrew her fingers slowly, bringing them up to lick so she could taste the woman. Sweet.

Always good to find a woman in excellent shape. All her flavors improved.

Tiffany rolled her weight away and let Wendra slide off the bunk, stripping the rest of the way naked before kneeling on the floor to pull a box from underneath.

Tiffany rolled over to watch, sneaking a kiss on the back of Wendra's neck that caused her to fumble the lock combination and have to start over.

Oops.

Tiffany slid just far enough away to watch the woman re-enter the combination and pop the lock open before flipping the lid up.

Bingo.

Tiffany hid the smile as she saw the giveaway on top, the soft pink uniform of the Tantric Legion, right down to the black mask that covered mouth and nose, and the round helmet it hooked to.

Princess Rayne was here and was hiding from everyone. That at least nailed down one salient point she and Dirk would need. And Tiffany had just cum her brains out.

She wondered if she needed to capture Wendra later for *questioning*. Maybe even *torture*. Or whatever she wanted to call it in the report she would file with her Timocracy superiors afterwards.

Wendra rooted around for a second and came up with

a cock in each hand. One was a traditional strap-on, with a flat base and cords to wrap around her thighs and waist. Black glass shaped like a cock, but long and slender enough that she might use it to take Wendra anally as well as vaginally.

The other was more interesting. At first glance, it looked like a tonfa, a nightclub with a bar on the side. But it was also cock shaped with an upwards curve. The other end, stuck out at ninety degrees, was a much thicker bulb, all in a hotter pink than the uniform.

"Have you been doing your kegel exercises?" Wendra looked up and asked with a saucy gleam in her eyes.

"Strapless?" Tiffany asked.

She suddenly realized that maybe she'd been missing something in her carnal adventures.

"Uh-huh," Wendra said, standing and dropping the other one into the locker. "This end goes inside you and this end goes inside me and you've got a cock to pound me with, but you're still a girl."

Tiffany clenched all her interior muscles once, just to see how sensitive everything was. Relaxing enough to handle a new toy being inserted, but she wondered if she would cum again from the tool, once everything got going.

"Oh, yum," Tiffany reached out to take it, and then moved to stand next to the woman.

She took the strapless dildo and spread her thighs enough to slip the bulbous end into her vagina, stretching everything just a little in spite of her overall looseness and relaxation, but it was thicker than even Dirk's impressive cock, maybe two and a half inches wide. It took a moment to find the right grip, and then she had a pink spike standing at attention.

"This what you needed?" she asked Wendra and watched the woman's eye squint as she licked her lips. "You should get it slick with your mouth."

Wendra dropped to her knees like a marionette whose cords had been cut. She reached both hands around to squeeze Tiffany's ass and opened her mouth to take a long, hard dildo in it. The surface had felt almost like flesh, so it would be like blowing a man, and Wendra went at it like a calf wanting fresh milk.

Tiffany felt the woman rocking on her cock and it got her warmed up all over again inside.

Wendra looked up with pleading eyes now, deep-throating the pseudocock.

"Pussy or ass?" she asked, just to watch those eyes roll back in pleasure.

Wendra backed off and swallowed.

"Pussy," she whispered. "First."

Tiffany nodded.

"Let's start boring then," she said with a grin.

She sat on the edge of the bed and gestured for Wendra to climb into her lap and impale herself.

Wendra smiled, then knelt again and reached between Tiffany's legs to fumble with the strapless device.

It had a vibrator inside, to top all the other magicalness Tiffany was filled with. The machine began to vibrate hard inside her, with a secondary circular motion of precession that felt like it might take half a minute to circle all the way around her vagina, pushing at every spot.

"Yes," Tiffany purred as Wendra stood again.

It took a little acrobatics to get the woman settled, but Wendra was so sloppy wet by now that the strapless dildo slipped right into her, all the way to the base with a hard groan of pleasure. She pulled her heels tight against Tiffany's bottom and squirmed rather than bouncing.

Wendra's hands went about Tiffany's back as she leaned in and began to suck on a nipple, going back and forth as Tiffany's hands kneaded Wendra's bottom.

Apparently the arousal was mutual, because Wendra started to writhe and gasp quickly, and had an orgasm less than a minute after she'd gotten penetrated.

But some days, you just needed to cum, and it didn't matter how you got there. Still, Tiffany held the woman in place and let the vibrator work on her, not letting Wendra escape that long, thick cock touching all the places that needed it.

Wendra wasn't a screamer. Instead she just chanted *fuck* under her breath like she was saying a rosary, never relenting as that orgasm just kept going.

Eventually her eyes opened and she whimpered, so Tiffany turned them onto their side and let Wendra collapse in a little ball of sweat and musk.

She almost started to cum again herself, but managed to find the off switch. After that, it was just a big cock inside her. As long as she didn't move, it wouldn't overstimulate anything, so she left it in and slipped around behind the other woman, just wrapping arms around her to hold her and keep her warm as she shivered from the aftermath.

"Fuck," Wendra murmured at one point, breaking the long stretch of silence.

"Needed that, did you?" Tiffany kissed her on the ear.

"You have no idea," Wendra gasped. "But I'm not sure I could handle that thing in my ass right now. I might just die from pleasure overload."

"I could always take a rain check," Tiffany murmured, her breasts pressed against the woman's back and her arms around her to feel the reaction to the word rain.

As in, Princess Rayne of Texas.

Wendra shuddered with a jolt of fear.

"How long will you and the girls be on the station, do you know?" Tiffany asked, slipping back into trade craft now, regardless of how much fun that had been, and might continue to be.

"No idea," Wendra whispered, her shudders slowly receding. "Boss doesn't tell us peons. Don't even have a comm that I could contact you."

Tiffany leaned in and kissed her cheek, hugging the woman tightly.

"Guess I'll just have to leave notes with the bartender and check if you have left me any?"

"I could probably do that," Wendra said. "Right now, I don't think I could walk, though."

"You curl up and sleep, then," Tiffany whispered in her ear. "I'll get dressed and go meet up with my friend and have a shower at her place."

"Okay."

Tiffany withdrew, and slowly eased that monstrous cock out, feeling empty now as she placed it atop the closed locker that contained the evidence she needed. Clothing had ended up everywhere, so it took her a bit to find it all and get dressed, feeling Wendra's sleepy eyes on her as she did a reverse striptease.

Dressed, Tiffany leaned over for a last kiss that was far more than just a peck, but she broke it before her body got her back in for another round with the woman.

"Thank you," Wendra whispered.

"Oh, thank you," Tiffany replied. "I haven't cum like that in a while and I've never used a strapless on someone before. Can't wait to try it again."

She held Wendra's hand briefly before slipping to the door and opening it, wondering it there would be a welcoming committee out there. Or armed troops who knew who she was.

But the corridor was empty.

Tiffany made her way back into the more public portions of the station, taking a long, circular route to make sure nobody was following her.

Fairly sure she was safe, Tiffany sent Ardel an update and then a simple note to Dirk

Tantric Legion confirmed.

What it all meant, she wasn't certain.

But it must be big.

Tiffany took a deep, wistful breath and headed back to her hotel room.

The game had just gotten interesting.

PRINCESS OF TEXAS

ABOARD THE JIRA SLEEPER SHIP
DR'GONAI ORBITAL

PRINCESS RAYNE STUDIED her reflection in the wrap-around mirrors as she emerged from her bath, water dripping from her perfectly-tanned body as she studied for any hint of aging. Lines. Sagging.

Anything that might suggest she wasn't twenty-two anymore.

She spent too much time, working mostly in secret, to maintain her diet as her metabolism changed, to work out enough with various machines that she kept her curves intact, neither grinding them off nor letting them sag. It wasn't nearly as easy as it had been sixteen years ago, but that was what it took.

As if if mattered, since Dirk hardly ever looked at her as anything but a problem, in spite of everything she did to still be hard, womanly, and inviting.

She laughed a little bitterly, alone in her space. Well, alone but for Panther, her latest bodyguard. But he was Jemhu, and rarely spoke. She found him more intimidating that way, as he stepped from the door with a freshly-warmed towel held out to wrap around her.

Panther adored her. Would always. His clan had owed her family loyalty for generations, and supplied many of the royal family's bodyguards.

Rayne looked up and smiled as she wrapped the towel around herself and he slid back into the shadows where his black fur and black uniform served to hide him. She had never fucked her bodyguards, but that was more about the cat-like nature of the species than anything.

The species had a cock like a Human, but it came with spines that extended when aroused, just like a house cat's, in order to hold the female in place while they mated. A Human woman didn't have the dermal pads in her vagina to not end up bleeding badly from such an act, and receiving pain had never been her thing.

Giving…Well, that was a different thing.

But he worshiped her like a goddess brought to Earth. In a way, she was, as her ancestors had uplifted the primitive Jemhu from bronze age barbarians to stellar age travelers generations ago, and his clan still took that bond seriously. Even going so far as to swear their clan to eternal service of hers, following when her ancestors had originally colonized the planet Texas.

It would not matter to Panther if she started to look her thirty-eight years. But it would to her.

Rayne was six feet tall and stood out, except when she was around beings as big as Panther. She was broad in the shoulders and hips, feminine but not girlie. Whatever the opposite of petite was.

All woman, but aging. There was no getting around it,

if she was going to be honest with at least herself. But still sexy, as long as she worked at it.

Already, she had had to add certain pills and creams on a daily basis. Time spent in the tanning booth religiously, just to never have a tanline of any kind. But she was still flexible enough that the lights could reach every spot and bronze it.

Other things kept her hair lush and wavy and black, down past her shoulder blades in a loose cut designed to frame her good looks in the right breeze.

Daily workouts with military precision to keep the muscles toned, even as she worked assiduously to keep breasts and hips full and enticing.

If she could ever capture the man's attention.

But Dirk was a free spirit, uninterested in turning into a Royal Consort. Hell, pretty soon, she'd be willing to just have him make contributions to a sperm bank, and she'd handle the rest herself.

She needed to entice that man. To have him. To feel that magnificent cock buried to the hilt inside her again and pulsing as he brought life and extended the royal line with the greatest genes available to the species.

Rayne knew his secrets. His past on Amaull as a candidate for the Timocracy. The ancient Human scholar Plato had once proposed a form of governance where philosopher-kings were raised from birth to rule, with an expectation that the best and brightest could be best found from all the broad testing. Texas was a monarchy, but Rayne understood that too many times in history such things had led to inbreeding problems, where cousins sought to conserve power by excluding the lower classes, rather than finding the man or woman with the best genes and getting them to contribute instead.

She needed Dirk. If she could have, she'd bear a sperm bank's worth of children with the man, just to give her heirs the edge over all of the rest of her family. And maybe the entire damned species.

And he was here. On this very ship. Images had confirmed it. Witnesses had looked at pictures. Others had known the man on sight.

She would have him.

Except that her first gambit had failed.

Rayne finished drying herself, dropped the towel on the floor for a maid and stepped into her main bedchamber, where Panther stood on one side, always vigilant, even when her visitor was only Jock Manhammer, Commander of the Tantric Legion.

She paraded her perfect nudity in front of the two men, just to see that little flare of lust come into Jock's eyes. She'd fucked the man a few times, but he had an ragged edge to his personality that would lead him to brutality if not contained, and she just wasn't into being a sub. Not for anyone but Dirk.

Two doms would never work out, but Jock could command her women with an iron fist and fuck them into submission, whenever one of his own lieutenants got out of hand.

Rayne occasionally even ordered it to occur space where she could watch secretly, pleasuring herself with both hands as Jock's Hammer got put to use on lesser pussies. She wondered if she'd need some sort of show in the short term, just to take off some of the edges that had been slicing at her recently.

It was like she could smell Dirk's sweat in the air system, filling her nose and licking at her pussy.

She smiled at Jock now and moved to the dresser. She bent like she always did, teasing the man. It almost felt tedious tonight. Too predictable, as she rooted around to find just the right panties in the bottom drawer. And did so in such a way that her perfect pussy was pointed right at the man, glistening and clean from her bath. Her breasts hung pendulous when she did, and she could almost hear the sound they made, slapping together like the right someone had her bent over like this and was hammering her from behind.

But not Jock. He always wanted to look you in the eyes when he fucked you. Okay, but not all that great, even with a cock like his.

Had they already descended into an unspoken Kabuki in their relationship?

She smiled over her shoulder as he stood at parade rest, possibly steaming. Jock always wanted to be in motion, like an attack dog sniffing and marking every border of his territory for intruders and threats. Rayne liked to take her time.

Next she selected a blade kilt. White leather belt wide enough to be called a girdle, hanging low around her broad hips to show off her wasp waist, with vertical strips of leather like sword blades hanging, each made of white leather edged in gold and with a blue gem at the tip for weight.

Rayne dithered for a moment before selecting the

matching bustier corset, also in white leather with gold. Blue as a contrast might have also worked, if she wanted a rhinestone bikini top cupping her full breasts and holding them in place. But then she'd have to have someone tie it and didn't feel like rewarding Jock with such personal closeness today.

She wrapped the bustier around herself and carefully settled each breast in place before hooking things closed and getting everything squished in just right.

A face crown completed this look, platinum frosted with real gold, resting atop her head with broad blades coming down to protect her cheekbones, like an ancient Hellenic warrior.

Finally, she was complete. Ready for visitors, who had been left waiting for long enough to perhaps grow nervous at what was coming next.

Rewards should be given quick and publicly, to secure the greatest value for the giver.

Punishments, on the other hand, should be a slow, patient process. Let the victim's mind do most of the work for you, as they sat outside the door to her personal chamber, shackled and hobbled.

Rayne took a deep breath as she turned back to Manhammer and nodded.

"Bring her in," she ordered bluntly.

Jock nodded and withdrew, leaving her alone but for Panther. Rayne took in the room and decided to sit in the main chair. The suite they had given her while on this ship was a bit cramped, at least compared to her personal chambers aboard *The Libertine*, where her bedroom was exactly an acre. Still, it was roomy enough for her current needs.

Bedspace on her right, where she could have up to eight in a good orgy, were she so inclined, up on a platform that would give the rest of the room a good vantage point if she needed an audience, or, more likely was part of one. Salon in the center, with long couches on each side and her chair, situated like a throne at the top of the square.

She thought about the thing that would become her throne one of these days, although Praise God that her father, King Zeric, might somehow managed immortality. Rayne couldn't think of anything worse than actually having to ascend the throne, back on Texas, and actually rule.

Unless she managed to find something here, first. To penetrate the Forbidden Triangle and master their secrets. That might make her Empress of entire sectors of space, rather than just one world.

If only her servants didn't fail her so often.

Two pink-clad troopers escorted Zamona in, hands on each elbow as the woman shuffled. Jock might have loosened the hobbles a few links, but she supposed he was even angrier at the woman's failure.

It had been an excellent plan, once Rayne's spies had confirmed that Dirk Thruster was aboard. An intercepted message to meet someone in a particular club, although that part had gotten garbled to the point she didn't know who he'd met.

But Zamona had been there, presenting genderqueer in a mannish suit as a lure to get Dirk's attention. You had to wave exotic under that man's nose as too many women just threw themselves at him and bounced off.

Rayne kept her grumbles on the topic to herself as Jock stood to one side, slightly ahead of Zamona as the two troopers held her in place. Rayne couldn't even reach down and stroke herself right now, much as she wanted to, thinking so much about Dirk.

Rayne needed anger front and center.

"You failed," she snapped flatly. "How?"

"He distracted me into thinking he had an accomplice behind him," Zamona replied carefully. "When I turned, he attacked, taking my pistol and knocking me into the elevator."

"And then he shot you and pressed the penthouse level for us to find you when you arrived," Rayne sneered.

"Yes, ma'am."

Rayne studied the woman, wondering if Zamona had finally gotten too old to be an effective honeypot. Or even a field agent. Perhaps the woman needed to be relegated to training new troopers and assassins now.

And that just frosted Rayne all the worse, staring at her former top assassin, as the woman was only two years older than she was. What did it say about Rayne? Was she getting too long in the tooth?

Was it finally time to grow up and start acting like management?

Ugh.

"So he knows your face and your shape," Rayne continued after a long stretch of internalized self-loathing. "Possibly your taste, since you did get him alone in a closet."

"Only for a kiss," Zamona spoke up for herself. "Nothing more. That was when I captured him initially, however briefly. Kissing."

Rayne ignored the woman now and turned to Jock, still standing at parade rest, square and upright, dark hair like Dirk's but kept short and professional.

"There were rumors that Dirk was seen with a female assistant of some sort?" she asked the man.

"Correct, but we don't have a good picture of her and nobody has seen her more recently to get a solid identification on the woman," he said.

"Could she be moving in disguise?" Rayne mused.

"Assumedly," Jock nodded.

Rayne turned her attention to Zamona again.

"Become someone else," she ordered. "Find the woman. Or locate Dirk's ship *Longsword* and wherever it is that his pilot Rico hid it. That's how you can rehabilitate your reputation now."

She waved a hand and the two troopers picked the woman up and bodily carried her from the room.

When they were alone, Rayne focused on Jock.

"I feel as though all our secrecy has already been wasted," she said. "Somehow, Dirk has stolen a march on us."

"He doesn't know what we're looking for," Jock replied helpfully.

"Only because we don't know," she snapped. "Lotus Blossom could mean anything, depending on how you want to translate it. All we know is that whatever it is will grant us access to the so-called Jade Gate that is apparently the only way into the Forbidden Triangle."

"Our other spies are still looking," Jock assured her.

"It may not be enough," Rayne grimaced.

"My Lady?"

"I may need to come onto the gameboard now," she said. "Instead of working quietly behind the scenes with my hands tied because nobody seems to be able to do their jobs when Dirk is involved."

"How can I serve?" he asked, mentally and emotionally stepping back now.

That was what she appreciated about Jock. The man was willing to shut up and take orders when his way hadn't worked and she had to step in.

"Have your aides leave all the briefing materials with me tonight," she decided. "I will review them and make a decision over breakfast. You may go."

Jock bowed and retreated, which was for the best. Rayne let her pique vent now, just cursing quietly as Panther moved to cover the only door and stand between her and any threat.

If only she could have convinced Dirk to stand there, none of this would be necessary.

Gods, she was so wound up even a long session with her biggest vibrator up her ass wasn't going to help.

Someone was going to pay for this.

———

RAYNE CLOSED the binder and considered the contents. The Forbidden Triangle. The Jade Gate. The Lotus Blossom.

Supposedly, paradise awaited the person who put the pieces together.

And someone had leaked enough to draw Dirk into the game, even before she would have.

How did that man always seem to know when to show up and thwart her?

Rayne sat in the middle of her bed and looked out over the space. Panther was out there in the dimness somewhere, unmoving but ever watchful as the innermost ring of her protectors. The Tantric Legion was mostly elsewhere, but she had an entire century of her women with her here should she need them.

She'd stripped all her gear back off and crawled into bed nude to read tonight, with only the light overhead on.

Rayne opened the binder again and pulled out the picture of Dirk that had been slipped in. She put the binder to one side and just studied the man. Square jaw they still called lantern in the modern age, framed with the mustache he generally retained. Longish hair so dark it was almost black, but she suspected that it would start coming in gray on the temples in another decade.

How much hotter would he look then?

This picture was taken at a moderate distance, outside when he wore a sort of kimono that showed off his muscles and that thick pelt of hair on his chest that she liked to run her fingers through.

Those long, thick sideburns. Not quite muttonchop but still framing his jaw nicely. The mustache that he let droop a little past his lips. Ticklish to kiss, or when he went down on her.

Shit. She was horny now.

Rayne moved to the edge of the bed and put the binder on the side table, opening a drawer to pull out the oil and a box with her various sex toys.

She opened it and looked at her options, from the smallest butt plug to a rubber dildo a horse might grow jealous of. Her pussy was growing damp, but she really felt it in her ass, so she grabbed the red vibrator.

Rayne paused and climbed out of bed for a towel to put down. Nothing she had would stain the sheets, but she didn't feel like sleeping in a wet spot tonight if Dirk hadn't been the source of the moisture.

She studied herself in the mirror again, half-light casting her in shadows. One hand lifted a breast, thumb and forefinger clamped lightly around a nipple, sending a jolt of electricity through her entire body.

Oh, yeah, she wasn't sleeping without an orgasm. Best make it a good one.

Back to bed, she laid out the towel and climbed into the center of it, oil in one hand and vibrator in the other. Pillows got arranged just so, and then she turned the vibrator on its lowest setting and laid it so it ran all the way up her lips and rested on her clit.

God, that felt good.

Rayne leaned back and let the hum fill her entire being as her eyes closed.

Entranced, she wondered what Panther thought, watching her from the shadows. She'd never asked how he might jack that lovely cock off, with spines like a thick crown just below the tip. There had to be a way.

She imagined his cock long and thick, like the man himself under that fur. Erect like an onyx pillar, a monument to lust that she might need to explore. Rayne filed a note to look up the species. She could wrap her lips around the tip, as long as she used her teeth to keep him from thrusting. Maybe both hands could find the tender spots along the shaft and work him until he flooded her mouth with hot cum?

Yes, but that wouldn't be enough. She'd need Dirk stretching her ass out at the same time.

Rayne lifted the vibrator and turned it off long enough to rub oil on the tip and shaft, slowly pumping it with her hand like it was a real cock that might just explode all over her if she did it right.

Below, she got wetter, so Rayne rolled onto her side and slipped an oil-covered finger into her ass as she got everything lubed. A second finger joined the first and she felt a jolt of lightning connect her fingers to her nipples, almost making her cum right then, but she wanted to be roasted on a cock spit first.

The vibrator got moved to the fourth setting and she pressed the tip against her anus, letting the press of the vibrations work their way into her.

Rayne relaxed and thrust, feeling it surge past the first ring of muscles and stop at the inner ring as she just laid on her side and let everything stretch.

The tool was shaped like a cock, but rounder. Curved upwards a little and made of metal that quickly warmed to her blood temperature. The head was as big as Dirk's, wider than it was tall, like a boar spear driving into her from behind as she held his head in the foyer.

Panther was out there in the darkness, invisible and watching. She put a finger in her mouth as though it was his cock and plunged Dirk's cock into her ass past the next ring of muscle. There was always a moment of pain that turned into pleasure as he filled her.

The base was tall and narrow, so it would slip between her cheeks and rest comfortably as Rayne rolled back over and sat up, feeling that cock almost seeming to touch her belly button from the inside as it sent waves of energy all through the entire inner structure of her clitoris and tapped on her g-spot like a caffeinated woodpecker.

Gods, yes.

Her eyes rolled back as she ground her hips down into the mattress, imagining Panther's cock in her mouth and Dirk's in her ass. Jock's rough hand came up and pinched her nipple now, gripping her entire breast as she visualized all three men taking her at once.

With what little bit was left of her mind, Rayne imagined rearranging everything now so Jock would be flat on his back, with her riding him as the third cock she needed to plug her every hole.

Fingers went down and teased her clitoris, but she was past teasing and just jammed two fingers into her pussy in the rhythm that she was bouncing herself on the bed. Three men, all at once. Big men with big cocks.

Taking her, whether she wanted or not, but Rayne knew she was still a princess. One safe word and they would all withdraw.

She controlled the fucking. Always.

She sucked. She fingered. She ground.

Three cocks in her mind, all growing heavier and thicker as the three men approached an orgasm that would leave her covered with cum and leaking from every hole like the little slut she wanted to be.

There.

Breathing stopped. Her heart was either racing so fast it was humming in harmony with the vibrator, or it had stopped.

Both hands came away from her body and gripped the towel and bed under her as a titanic earthquake built outwards from Dirk's magnificent cock in her ass. Richter seven. Eight.

NINE.

She came, thrashing madly, her moaning almost a scream to lift the rafters in here before everything just completely overwhelmed her.

The vibrator in her ass suddenly hurt, and Rayne plucked it out quickly, turning it off and dropping it on the towel next to her as she started to breathe again.

Her fingers ached from clawing at the bedding, so she relaxed them as well, rolling onto her side and whimpering for a few moments as she recovered, almost drooling on Dirk's picture as she opened her eyes and managed to focus on his face.

Tenderly, Rayne pulled the picture close and kissed it, wishing she had the real thing here to hold her.

Soon, though.

Soon, she would penetrate the Forbidden Triangle and all things would be possible.

RAYNE EMERGED from her morning toilet refreshed and almost hyper with excitement after an amazing orgasm and a good night's sleep. Jock was there, dressed in a civilian suit today rather than his vaguely military-looking outfit from yesterday.

She sat in the chair she thought of has her throne and gestured him to join her instead of lurking overhead. He moved quickly and studied her face.

"You are committed to appearing on the decks?" he asked, as if he could read the answer in her eyes.

"I am," Rayne nodded. "You and Panther would stand out too much, so I need to take a few of the girls with me. Not Zamona, since Dirk knows her."

"He knows you," Jock pointed out.

"First thing today, I made an appointment at a spa," Rayne informed the man. "I had considered trying to appear as a Trillo, or a L'Quene. Possibly even a Shydrun, but I think I simply need to remain Human, but a different kind of Human."

"Oh?" Jock asked, as if envisioning her as someone else.

"Pale skin, even though I work so hard on my tan," she simpered. "Reddish-auburn hair and straight. Possibly even shorter like that one agent that's helped Dirk a few times. What was her name?"

"*Tits* McGee," Jock informed her.

Rayne heard a hard growl under Jock's words and wondered if he'd tried to bed the woman and either been cock blocked somehow, or she'd somehow fucked him into submission. Rayne wasn't sure how that could be done, but there was embarrassment and anger there that she might need to explore sometime.

Maybe secretly send a message directly to McGee and start corresponding with the woman like pen pals, just to find out how she'd defeated Jock Manhammer in bed?

Rayne smiled but kept the evil knowledge out of her eyes.

"Yes," she said instead. "Her. Dirk seems to favor the woman. Perhaps a case of mistaken identity would draw him into a trap."

"Dirk Thruster is a sidebar," Jock reminded her. "We seek the Lotus Blossom."

"Indeed, but he also needs to be subdued somehow," Rayne said. "Unless you plan on seducing the man yourself and fucking his secrets out of him."

"That doesn't work," Jock informed her. "Dirk's not into pillow talk that way. At least, he never was in the past."

Rayne didn't press. Like Dirk, Jock had once been a candidate for the Timocracy, raised as a potential Philosopher-King, but he had washed out fairly late in the game, whereas Dirk had simply chosen to leave at the very end, rather than ascend. As far as she'd been able to find out, no other candidate besides Dirk had ever been offered a space in the Timocracy and not accepted it.

But Dirk always stood out as special, no matter the room full of people you might put him in.

Rayne drew a careful breath, wondering what it might be like to just sit in a chair nearby, pleasuring herself while watching Dirk and Jock fuck each other. That might be tonight's fantasy, as she envisioned the man before her.

"So, I will have them turn me into *Tits* McGee for now," Rayne said to the man. "I'll work the older parts of the station, since the rumors and legends seem to go back that far."

"I do not believe those myths that the colonists who originally came to Dr'Gonai subsequently went into the Forbidden Triangle," Jock said flatly. "The barriers were already in place before then."

"You continue your mission, General," Rayne snapped. "I will take one bodyguard with me as a BFF and we will explore other options. Questions?"

"No, Princess," Jock surrendered, as she knew he would.

The man was a pushover around her, and she knew it. Rayne just had to be careful not to push too much, lest he figure out his weak spots against her and somehow armor them.

If only he wasn't so rough in bed.

RAYNE STUDIED her face in the mirror. In addition to red hair, the fabulously gay man at the spa had stood her up nude in front of a blank wall and shot her with a kind of squirt gun/misting tool that was filled with something like henna, giving her freckles from her ribs up. Shading on her cheekbones and jaw had made her face more slender, and he had instructed her to keep her hair pulled back on the sides into a clip but looser on top, to the point that her entire face looked more aquiline as a result.

He'd even added some scarlet henna to her areola to

make them much darker for a few weeks, in case she needed to go topless. And then he'd waxed her pubic hair entirely, leaving her completely bare down there, something that she'd told him she'd never done.

The man had looked at her and smiled.

"Stupid fucker won't even know it's you until you get his cock inside you," he'd said, dead serious. "I can't do anything about him recognizing the feel of your pussy, so maybe you should get him a little drunk first, and double your kegel routine for a few weeks."

She'd stared at the man open mouthed, but he'd only smiled.

"Darling, many women come to me in order to become someone else, even for just a few weeks," he'd said. "The best revenge in the universe is fucking his best friend in disguise. Second best is fucking him."

The way he'd said it suggested experience on the topic, so Rayne had gone with it and worked on becoming a different woman.

Rayne took a deep breath as she and her new BFF sidekick bodyguard were about to enter what her mind kept wanting to interpret as an Arabic souq, the ancient marketplace at the center of town. God knew the *Jira Sleeper Ship* was so huge that it constituted a city in orbital space, but she'd only ever been in the Casino areas, rather than moving down to the other places, well below the domes, where the lower deck people lived.

It was cramped here.

Steffy had instructed her to wear tight clothes, so hands could not touch without her knowing it. Could not pick pockets easily. Both women had knives and nervefire pistols, both highly illegal, but she was a Princess, and could always play that card if the authorities got involved.

Lots of folks went slumming on this station, after all. She just had a reason.

Steffy had wanted to lead, but didn't know where they were going, and needed to watch her back, so the tall woman remained a pace behind her.

Certainly, the woman would not keep a low profile, as she stood six feet three tall and obviously worked with heavy iron on a regular basis, and probably a variety of artificial chemicals to get that broad chest, muscles stacked on muscles while still having breasts. Cords running under the skin of her arms like wires.

Rayne wondered if the woman's clitoris was in the process of turning into a penis, something large enough to suck on like a thumb. She might ask at some point. Maybe inspect it personally.

They both wore long slacks and good boots today. Undershirts and tunics long enough to cover bottoms. Rayne had been iffy, but Jock had insisted, and once they passed into this section, she understood. They kept it air in here chilled enough that her nipples would have been standing out against a single layer.

The lighting was also bad. Well, worse. Half as much, as if the station authorities were meeting some legal minimum, instead of making the space welcoming, like the casino and resort decks above. Hallways seemed minimal as well, with shops that crept out into them, to the point that she would be brushing up against strangers or bulkheads with every step.

And the smell of unwashed bodies threatened to

overwhelm her. At least there wasn't any sort of a wet market, adding the smell of fear and shit from animals awaiting their turn in the dinner pot, or that might be too much to handle.

But all the information suggested that the underdecks held the secret. So Rayne had ready cash in her pocket, opposite the pistol she hoped not to have to fire. Possibly Jock had instructed Zamona to shadow them, since both he and Panther would stand out.

She plunged into the souq with a shallow breath, wondering if a cloth across her face, marking her as an outsider, would be more trouble than just breathing yuck.

First stop was a coffee shop that her agents had suggested was a place for information. Rayne wallowed in the pleasant smell of roasted beans as she entered with Steffy on her heels, and they made their way to a side table.

She wasn't sure if you still called the man a publican when she didn't serve alcohol. Whatever he was called, a short, fat Human waddled close, bearing two mugs in one hand and a chipped porcelain pot in the other. Rayne left a handful of coins on the table. Far more than covered their time.

"Food, perhaps?" he asked in a raspy tone.

"Perhaps," Rayne eyed him closer. "Information would be even more helpful. Who should we seek with questions?"

As he stewed, Rayne swept up all the coins and put them into his unresisting hand, closing it up and smiling.

"I will inquire," he nodded deeply after a moment and withdrew.

Rayne counted that as a win. Her intelligence had suggested this place as a starting point, but nobody had ever really gotten deep enough in the local culture to know the truth. And he had not asked if she sought a person, an item, or just information, so hopefully he would watch her for a while, and then pass a word.

Surely, the man had a cousin. They all had cousins. One of them had probably perked up in a nearby chamber for reasons he could not even identify.

She settled back into the wall and sipped the coffee. Roasted dark but recently, so that it hadn't faded down to just burned, like it would be after a few days. Far better than she might have expected, looking around.

The room was small, with a low ceiling that probably hung ominously over any of the taller species, or even tall Humans. The lighting was low, but it looked more a statement of ambiance, rather than the poverty outside. They were aboard a ship in orbit, or she might have expected a couple of hookahs in one corner, filling the air with a fog of rich tobacco smoke cut with traces of other things.

Three other tables were occupied. One by a single man busily typing away in a manner that suggested the archetypal novelist in a coffee shop. A second by a pair of older women who looked like neighborhood gossips from the way they stole glances at Rayne and Steffy. The last table held what she guessed was an insurance salesman with a husband and wife couple, voices low and heads together.

It was weird, without pomp surrounding her. Rayne rarely managed to escape Jock and his firm grip on where she could go without adult supervision. It was almost as bad as being home on Texas some days.

Maybe she needed to ditch the Tantric Legion from time to time and find her way around in mufti? Princess and the Pauper? Was that what she'd been doing wrong for all these years? Certainly, today was radically different, in a world of sameness.

She smiled at Steffy and leaned close so they could talk like girls, rather than boss and bodyguard. Wouldn't do to give the whole game away to strangers watching.

"So do you prefer girls or boys?" Rayne murmured as the tall woman leaned in.

Steffy thought about it for a long moment, but she'd been warned that conversations could get strange where Rayne was concerned.

"Girls with available cocks," Steffy said quietly. "I like a good fucking occasionally, but too few men know how to use their tongues and fingers."

Rayne nodded sagely.

"Dirk's one," she assured the woman. "Rico, too, if we can figure out where he's hiding."

"Thruster's mechanic?" Steffy asked, a bit surprised. "I heard he wasn't as good."

"Nobody is as good as Dirk Thruster," Rayne said. "Man, woman, or ambiguous, mesomorphic alien. Rico's still pretty damned good, if you ever get a chance to ride him like a pony."

"Noted," Steffy said. "Importance?"

"Two outsiders, slumming," Rayne nodded to the room. "We might be on the prowl for sexual shenanigans and looking for a more interesting brothel than the resorts keep."

"Wouldn't those sorts of places be more exotic?"

"Yes, but they still have to keep things pretty vanilla, at least from a legal perspective. We're looking for trouble down here. New thrills that we can't get upstairs."

"And you brought a musclebabe in case you run into trouble," Steffy said with a quick grin.

"Or we find a bare knuckles boxing arena and I can put you up against one of the local bruisers," Rayne grinned. "Anything's possible when you slide out of the spotlight and into the shadows."

The smile that came over the woman's face was telling. Rayne had learned a long time ago that the men with sharply-cut muscles and hard definition were all show ponies. Good on a stage as part of a cheesecake competition, but slow and awkward when it came time for violence.

The men with a bit of a gut, and an extra layer of fat everywhere, those were the dangerous ones. The lifters that looked like fire plugs all sloping muscles. Morgan horses instead of Thoroughbreds.

She'd instructed Jock to find her a woman who looked big and rough. Certainly, the Legion had a selection of ninjas. Small, fast, discrete, and deadly.

Rayne had asked for an orc who wasn't ugly. Brown-haired Steffy wasn't beautiful, but partly that was the way the steroids and other things gave her a bit of a mannish appearance. She probably took other pills and creams to keep hair from growing on her jaw and chest, but she had hips and breasts still.

Rayne planned to taste her at some point, just because.

However, for now they were just a pair of tourists in the seedier part of the ship. Not that the locals would see it that way, but down here you found two meter hallways instead of four. Two and a half meter ceilings instead of three to five. Compact and cheap, because you had to have these people as a service sector, but didn't pay them well enough to live nice.

To Rayne, that was a silly mistake. The resorts and casinos made so much money that they could have turned the lower decks into the exact same flats as tourists had. In fact, it cost more to design two architectures. In the end, she supposed that people wanted someone to look down on.

Stupid, but behavior like that always allowed her to meet recruiting goals for the Legion, when she could offer young women a way out of a place like this and a leg up to something better in life, if they were smart and saved their pay to supplement retirement money.

Just because, she reached out and pulled Steffy's head close enough to kiss the woman once, glancing around to see who flinched in outrage or voyeurism. Steffy tasted nice. Kissed nice.

Rayne sat back and sipped her coffee. Steffy squirmed a little and did the same, obviously trying to stay tough and hard, even as she wanted to be a little girlie. She was a trooper given a chance to shine before the boss.

The publican had vanished before. He returned now and stepped close with a pot in hand. He swapped the old pot with a new one and Rayne noted a piece of paper mostly hidden under the new one. She nodded to the man and watched him withdraw.

She refilled her cup and palmed the paper. Steffy also got some. They sat and drank for a time before standing and heading out, an extra tip on the table as a thank you, in case they returned later.

Rayne headed out and found a side corridor that was mostly empty, She turned into a corner and let Steffy keep watch as she opened the note and read the message It was an address, down another level, deeper into the area she thought of as the souq.

Hopefully, leading them to someone who knew things.

RAYNE STUDIED the shop from down the corridor and across the way. This space was actually more open, with the main corridor five meters wide, though interrupted by tables stuck out in front of shops and shopkeepers seated at them watching. The ceiling was three meters, and the lighting was better.

She wondered if that first level was intended to convey *seedy* to the tourists who didn't know any better, giving them an extra bit of adventure on the wrong side of town, as it were. Down here, it was more like a small town station, where there wasn't great wealth, but also not great poverty.

Her target was a psychic. Weird, but Rayne supposed the such a person might have to have great personal skills and contacts with a variety of locals. Better than a woman who arranged marriages, although probably not as connected.

Rayne nodded to her shadow and stepped forward, ducking her head under the lintel and entering as a chime announced her existence. A second ring sounded for Steffy.

The inside felt like a bad B-movie. Those cheesy ones you found in the middle of the night when you staggered home from some party, too wound up to sleep, but done with people. Shelves on all sides covered with strange bric-a-brac she could not identify. There was almost no free space on the walls. The floor under her feet had transitioned from metal decks to a thick rug.

Cases on three sides were fronted with glass and contained tarot decks, crystals, small knives that were not that sharp, and glass spheres on wooden tripods.

A woman emerged from the back, wearing dark robes over a heavy-set figure. Short, almost squat. Dark hair, but dyed badly to a monochromatic black that was as artificial as her eyebrows. Only the maze of wrinkles on her face were real.

"How may I be of service?" the old crone asked in a voice already tired of dealing with tourists who had wandered into the wrong shop.

"We stopped at a coffee shop up a level," Rayne replied, showing her the piece of paper. "I was sent to see you, I believe."

A claw came out and took the paper from Rayne's hand. The old woman pulled it close and read it without reaching for the reading glasses she needed. She looked up after a moment with a scowl.

"What is it you seek?" she asked.

"Are you Imelda?" Rayne asked, referring to the name on the page.

"I am," she replied.

"Then I might be on something of a scavenger hunt," Rayne said.

Imelda studied the two of them for a long moment and then gestured them to follow her as she stepped into the next room.

This was a séance room. No other word described it. Even thicker rug under foot, possibly black but the light was too low in here to know for certain. Curtains hanging from all the walls, but what they obscured wouldn't be obvious until someone moved them to look.

Imelda moved behind a table and pointed to two chair in front. Rayne sat. Steffy joined her a moment later.

Hard wood under her bottom. Not cold, so someone had been here recently enough to warm it.

The table was covered over with a white cloth, a little rough under her arms as Rayne leaned forward to study the old woman who watched her with such bright eyes, dark though they were.

"Does he love the woman whose visage you wear?" Imelda asked suddenly, jarring Rayne sideways.

"He loves all women," she managed to stammer in response. "Some more than others. Perhaps her more than me. But that's not why I did this."

"Oh?"

"She looks like another now as well, I think," Rayne continued. "But that inspired me to hide in plain sight, because I do not look like the woman he expects."

"And you hide from him?"

"I seek a thing," Rayne said. "A sign. Perhaps a person. Or even a legend that has drawn me across the light-years to Dr'Gonai and the *Jira Sleeper Ship*. But I think it is older than the casinos."

"Indeed?" Imelda asked quietly. "Dr'Gonai is old but not ancient. The colonists came from elsewhere."

"And some may have gone on," Rayne said. "I heard a fragment of a story that suggested a way to penetrate the Forbidden Triangle by way of something called the Jade Gate. And a guardian that protected the gates. Or an item. The Lotus Blossom."

Imelda leaned back now and those hard eyes studied the two of them, but only long enough to discount Steffy for what she was, muscle protecting Rayne.

Imelda zeroed in on Rayne.

"Truly a dangerous quest, then," she said simply. "Many have sought, but none, to the best of my recollection have ever returned, of the few who were successful."

"But they were successful?" Rayne pressed.

"So the legends say," Imelda nodded quietly. "Are you prepared to pay the price for such knowledge?"

Rayne staggered there, at least in her mind.

The spoiled, bratty Princess was a role she played, much of the time to get people to underestimate her. But at times, she sometimes forgot that she had a brain and had to turn it back on.

It was sometimes a little too seductive to let King Zeric rule and have Jock Manhammer run things in the Tantric Legion for her. No responsibilities but pleasure.

Hobbies half-started and abandoned when her squirrel mind found something else bright and shiny instead.

"What price?" she asked with a little bit of gasp to her breath, already feeling an uncomfortable weight take hold behind her belly button.

Cold and heavy, like the kind of bad meal where she had the chef exiled afterwards.

The old woman seemed to sense it. Or smell fear.

"Possibly only your life," she said. "Most likely your soul."

Rayne grimaced. Ninety nine times in a hundred, or even more, she would normally walk away at that sort of talk. Or find a way to send someone else in her stead.

But this was the Forbidden Triangle. Who knew what magical power or wealth might be hers for the asking, once she found her way inside?

There was nobody Princess Rayne Summers of Texas trusted to be handed that sort of power and then bring it back to her like a good little servant.

The old woman smiled at her now. It was cold and brittle. Unfriendly, with a hint of triumph.

Yet another person who thought the Princess was too spoiled to make the hard decisions? Lost in herself and chasing after dreams that were more in line with her at eighteen, rather than thirty-eight?

But what did she really have to lose at this point? She would hit forty soon, and probably have to admit defeat.

Or worse, grow up.

Fuck that noise.

"I would have one more grand adventure first," Rayne said to the woman, her chin coming up.

Imelda nodded, as if she'd been listening to that same internal monologue.

Rayne hoped she wasn't muttering. That would just make it worse.

"Then this is the time," Imelda said. "If you would walk that path, you should take a moment to steel yourself. Pack an overnight bag, both of you, and dress for planetary conditions that are not all that harsh, but not paradise, either. A messenger will arrive for the two of you, tomorrow at dawn, and you two *alone*."

Rayne recognized a dismissal when she heard one. She rose. Steffy bounced up a moment later, somewhat lost, but doing her job.

Rayne made it to the door when she realized that she had not told this old woman who she was, or where she could be found. She had not even paid her for the information. And yet Rayne had no doubts about a knock on her door in the morning.

"I'm not afraid of you," she said to the woman, hoping that speaking the words out loud would make them truth.

Imelda the wizened Crone smiled at her.

"You will be," she said simply. "You will be."

RAYNE STOPPED at a bar on the casino deck as she made her way back into what her mind kept interpreting as sunlight. Or whatever it was you wanted to use to describe what had just happened. Felt like she had just walked out of somebody's definition of hell. At least Steffy looked just as ragged.

"I feel kinda dumb some days," her bodyguard began as they sat at a table away from everyone else in the middle of the space. "But what the hell happened down there?"

Rayne fixed the big woman with a steady eye.

"That explanation depends on whether or not you believe in magic," Rayne said starkly.

At least Steffy flinched as much as Rayne wanted to.

"Option one, Imelda had enough spies in her network to know who I was before I even arrived in her shop," Rayne explained. "And that that whole thing was a performance to make me nervous, which it did."

"Or two?" Steffy asked nervously.

"Or two, we just met one of the beings who normally reside inside the Forbidden Triangle, and that might have been as close as either of us are likely to get to meeting a god. I need something to drink. You should have something as well, assuming it won't mess with your other chemicals."

"I should be good," Steffy stuttered a little. "As long as it's not tequila."

Rayne nodded and made a certain type of eye contact that drew the female bartender close to this end, eyes open expectantly.

"One and One for both of us," she said, letting some of her stress show as she gestured.

The woman nodded sympathetically and went to work.

Rayne dropped more coins on the table and released a big sigh.

The bartender was fast. She came around the end of

the bar with two pint glasses of brown, and a pair of shot glassed filled with caramel gold.

"Four," she said as she served them, but Rayne handed her ten coin and sent her on her way with a smile.

She and Steffy picked up the shots of whiskey and toasted themselves with a clink before hammering the glasses empty and banging them on the table in unison.

Both reached for the ale and began to sip.

For Rayne, she wasn't sure which of those two options —spies or gods—frightened her more right now. There was probably a third and a fourth option she wasn't thinking of right at the moment. Certainly, the people at the spa would have her name and appearance, and could have dropped that into the river of gossip. Or someone recognized her at the coffee shop.

This was a resort and casino ship, even though *Jira* was more like a city in space. There were any number of folks doing menial jobs that were normally invisible, unless you were paranoid enough to track them closely. Jock might have. Rayne had not.

Rayne felt eyes on her as she took a second drink. The ale was malted instead of hopped, so it went down almost as smooth as the whiskey had, which was good.

A man, on the far corner of the bar. Looked like a Lothario, but wasn't that old. Dressed in nice slacks and an indoor jacket over a shirt, all in shades of dark red that worked well. Still, he certainly felt like the kind of cad who seduced women with false promises and pretty lies, just from the small smile on his face as he looked her over, possibly thinking he was looking at the real Tits McGee.

As a Princess, Rayne had run into more than her number of such punks, and developed a sense for them.

Not bad looking. Thirty, to round it one way or the other. Pretty in a way that would pale badly as he aged. Not like that grim ruggedness that men like Dirk or Rico had to look forward to, the one that would still have women getting wet just looking at them when they were old men with white hair.

Fool took her appraising look as an invitation. Picked up his glass with a jaunty smile and strutted over to their table.

Tall and lean, except that as he got close, it looked like average and lean, just appearing taller. Steffy probably looked down one him from about four inches, even barefoot, depending on the heels on his feet.

Smelled pretty. Rayne did have to give him that. And points for audacity, to walk up on two of them with seduction in mind.

"Ladies…" he said brightly, but Rayne cut him off.

"Unless all you're looking for is a quick hand job in a quiet corridor, you're wasting your time, bucko" she replied equally chipper. "I've had a long day and run out of patience for stupid bullshit."

She nearly laughed when Steffy just stood up and loomed over the man. Maybe six inches, then, meaning Rayne would have three on him.

"And unless you've got a cock that would make a horse jealous," Steffy sort of growled, "I'm not even sure I'd even feel it going in."

Punk turned a little white, but didn't immediately run like hell, so Rayne had to give him points for that as well.

Just kind of stood there and recalibrated everything as Rayne watched him.

Must have had more beer in him than was probably smart, because he sneered.

"So how much will a handjob cost me?" he asked in a low, huffy voice, turned to focus on Rayne and trying to pretend that someone hadn't just put up a building behind him.

Rayne caught Steffy's look of outrage but shook her off from beating the stupid fucker to death. Not that he probably didn't deserve it. Heaven forbid.

But it had already been a day. And fuck it, why not take the crazy all the way down into weird? Hadn't she just been talking about meeting gods? Maybe one had decided to test her?

Weirder shit was likely to happen before all this was over.

"Three hundred," she replied disinterestedly. "Five hundred if you want to cum on my tits."

Double and more the going rate. Good enough to make this stupid shit stomp off in a huff and bother someone else.

Except he stared at her. Not with recognition. Lust, maybe. Like he could see through the makeup at the woman underneath.

Or he had fetish for freckled redheads with big tits. There was always that.

Rayne caught the grumble under his breath about highway robbery before he snarled at her.

"Fine," he said angrily. "Where?"

Rayne stared at him for a good three seconds before

she picked up her beer and drained it. Wasn't going down on the boy, but a little liquid courage never hurt. Steffy quickly reached down and did the same, but there was a wall of utter shock in that girl's eyes.

Or course, most of the Legion preferred girls. That was one of the recruiting bars you had to clear to join, after all, going down on one of the Legionnaires to prove your sexuality was fluid enough to fit in with a lesbian strike force.

Rayne couldn't even believe herself when she stood up, right into that boy's space. He really was only about five foot nine, upon reflection, so she had three inches on him. Three intimidating inches. Plus, broader shoulders.

She put a hand on his chest, but didn't shove.

"No kissing," she informed him. "That costs extra. Blowjob starts at a thousand."

"Whatever," he replied in a snotty tone.

Oh, what the hell?

Rayne turned towards the front door and started walking.

"This way," she said over her shoulder, glancing to make sure Steffy was following him, just for the extra adventure.

Steffy probably outweighed the boy. Rayne was close, but hers was all curves and boobs, instead of lats and thighs on her BFF.

Out the door, Rayne turned right and quickly went through a door into a stairwell. Normally good enough, but this was the main deck and too busy for her tastes, so she went up a level into the space that was more of a mezzanine around some of the open spaces, hanging out over the vaulted ceiling areas over some of the gaming floors.

She'd found a quiet spot early on to watch the flow of sentient beings without necessarily being visible, so Rayne headed that direction, wondering at what point pretty boy behind her would change his mind.

After all, a quiet space for a handjob might also be the perfect place for a bodybuilder babe like Steffy to mug him.

Not that Rayne had planned anything like that walking down here.

Planned.

They emerged onto a long balcony that dead-ended over a kind of market square, but the place was currently closed, as it was more of a night market for when the tourists and high-rollers were on the prowl.

Rayne walked along to the end and turned to lean against the railing.

"You there," she said, pointing back into something of a blind spot formed by a pillar and a kink in the bulkhead around some air shafts.

Pretty boy backed himself into the space a little awkwardly and maybe just a hint nervous. Steffy was close enough that anybody walking down to talk to them would only see her back. And there was no place he could really run at this point, if shit went sideways, unless he wanted to go over a second story railing.

Rayne stepped close enough to press her breasts against his chest.

"So," she smiled down at him and spoke in a husky voice. "You wanna cum on my tits, or just have me jack you off onto whoever happens to be walking below when you go?"

For extra fun, she ground her groin against his thigh as she spoke, licking her lips and moaning a little, like maybe she was getting off on the scene.

Sexual agency was something Rayne always found arousing, and Pretty Boy here was about to literally put his dick in her hands. That or run off screaming.

Either way, she won.

"Tits," he kind of gasped, still trying to find his footing.

Rayne probably should have known better than setting a Fuck You price without knowing how much this idiot was willing to spend, but she was here, and it was maybe a little too much fun watching him squirm.

"Tits?" she purred at him, reaching down and fondling the man through his pants for a moment. "Okay. Show me the cash."

He reached up after flinching backwards into the wall behind him. Pulled out a wallet and withdrew five bills that he showed her before sticking the money in the outside pocket of his jacket.

Rayne had her back to most of the arena, so she reached up and pulled her shirt open both ways, letting her breasts hang over the cloth and pinching both of her nipples a little just to warm them up. The shirt was soft, but she'd gotten a little moist on the walk over here, just thinking about something so outrageous as giving a total stranger a handjob in a public place, however private this corner might be.

His way eyes lit up as she knelt made Rayne think he

might need to visit to a shrink, but maybe he already had done so, and had already identified his particular kink. And it wasn't like it was that hard for a woman to change her tan, her freckles, and her boobs, if someone else was willing to pay enough to frost them regularly.

She reached out again and fondled him, even as she licked her lips in anticipation. Certainly, he was already larger than she had been expecting.

One hand opened the seal and the other pulled him out. Not as long as Dirk. Not as thick. Uncut, so she wrapped her hand around his foreskin and pulled it back with all her fingers, like he was fucking her hand.

Turned out that it was a nice cock, and it got longer as she slowly pumped it. She'd been expecting three inches and he was already going past six now.

Behind her, she heard Steffy gasp in surprise.

Rayne smiled now and took him in an overhand grip, the eye staring right at her and already starting to leak a little fluid. Rayne leaned forward suddenly and licked the tip, just to taste this stranger before he could react.

Not bad. Obviously ate healthy and got the right amount of exercise, but he wasn't paying enough to cum in her mouth or on her face, so she leaned back again and started to play with her right nipple as her right hand continued pumping.

Pretty Boy started to moan under his breath and his eye lids got fluttery as Rayne looked up at him, locking the eye contact as she jacked him off before she even knew his name.

Steffy surprised Rayne by stepping close and leaning over enough to whisper to the man.

"Maybe some other time, you could put that long, hard thing between my tits," Steffy growled quietly at him. "And just let me go up and down on your cock, squeezing them together like my friend's hand. Warm and tight and inviting, just like her pussy would be, but you'd be so close that maybe I open my mouth and you shoot your load into it. Or paint my face. Mmmmm. Yeah. I can taste your cum. Feel it dripping down my chin. Hot and sweet and..."

She stopped there, but that was fine. He'd been staring down at Rayne's tits until Steffy got into his mind and his eyes rolled back in his head. That long cock got thicker as she pumped, and then suddenly he spasmed hard in her hand.

Rayne leaned back a little and pointed his cock down, holding it just a few inches from her breast, because he was already close.

And then he was there. Blasted her once, twice.

Rayne slowed her pace down and got a third little spurt out of him as his legs buckled.

She caught all his semen in her other hand, letting it run down onto her palm as he gasped.

Steffy surprised her by reaching down and lifting her hand up to suck all the juice off her palm and then lick it clean.

Then she leaned into the man and smiled as she pulled the money out of his pocket and handed it to Rayne.

"Next time, I'll might even give you a discount on the blowjob," Steffy smiled, her other hand pulling Rayne to her feet and sending her back down the walkway.

Rayne looked back as she walked, with her kinkierthan-expected bodyguard following as she pulled her shirt closed again, only a little sticky. Pretty Boy was still a frozen statue with a half-rigid cock just dangling out of his pants as they reached the door, but he wasn't following.

She'd need a shower when she got back to the room, but that was fine. Maybe she'd drag Steffy into the water with her and make it a two-fer.

"That was interesting," she murmured to Steffy as they got into the stairwell and headed up.

Two levels up on a landy, Steffy finally spoke.

"Worked in a call center when I was sixteen," the woman laughed with a girly voice so at odds with her otherwise mannish silhouette. "One of *those* jobs. Didn't really like boys, but was really good at getting old men off when they called in. The Legion pays way better and I don't have to deal with icky pervs."

"How about horny princesses?" Rayne asked. "He had a nicer cock than I was expecting."

"Me, too," Steffy said quietly. "Considered sucking on it, but he hadn't paid for the privilege, and obviously had the money. Next time."

"Gonna go trolling for pin money?" Rayne laughed.

"Bet I could get him to lick me pretty good, if I pinned him down by sitting on his face while you were riding him," Steffy laughed back. "Shit, I'm horny now."

"We'll take care of that when we get back to the room," Rayne promised.

"Why wait?" Steffy asked, reaching out a hand to stop Rayne and turn her sideways. "After all, your tits are still sticky. Someone should do something about that."

Before Rayne could react, Steffy bent down and pulled

Rayne's shirt open again. She leaned in and kissed a nipple, causing Rayne to moan a little. Steffy's tongue wasn't as rough as a cat's but it felt like a warm towel as it got stuck in Rayne's belly button. Then small kisses and licks, covering every part of her stomach that might have Pretty Boy's cum on. Or was even remotely at risk of being messy.

Rayne felt her pussy get wet now, but they were in a public stairwell.

Or maybe it was the thought of another total stranger suddenly walking up and watching them?

Steffy finally got back up to a nipple and took extra care, working her way all the way around, lifting the breast to get underneath and still pinching the nipple just exactly the right amount to make Rayne start to writhe a little.

Then Steffy switched hands and breasts, and Rayne got the other side equally cared for. She was still sticky as Steffy stood up and closed her shirt, a shit-eating grin on the woman's face as she leaned close and they kissed.

It was a long, hot kiss, arms around each other and right legs both forward to give the other woman a fulcrum to grind her clit and pussy against. At some point, a group of tourists walked by, gasping and then harrumphing angrily. Sounded like Dad, Mom, and two children that were old enough to understand what they were seeing. Mom had to scold the son and daughter, and then drag Dad off when he wanted to stay and watch the lesbians put on a floor show.

Rayne wondered if she should slum more, just so she could make a little cash on the side as she discovered she might be a greater exhibitionist than she'd realized.

Eventually, they were alone and broke the hug.

She took Steffy's hand and started back up the stairs, looking forward to seeing what kind of clit those various chemicals might have given the woman. And how sensitive it was to the kiss.

She was going to need to taste Steffy tonight.

Because tomorrow, Rayne just knew things were going to get weirder.

Someone was going to knock on her door. And she'd be going with them.

RAYNE'S QUEST

PRINCESS RAYNE FLINCHED when the door to her entertaining salon opened and one of the soldiers of her Tantric Legion entered nervously. The trooper made eye contact with Jock Manhammer first, her commander; then glanced at Steffy, Rayne's bodyguard sidekick, seated nearby in mufti.

Finally, the woman screwed up her courage to look at Rayne herself.

"Princess, you have a visitor," she said simply.

"We will join you shortly," Rayne said gravely, nodding and waving the woman back out of the room.

Jock had been standing to one side at parade rest, as if having his hands behind him made the angry flexing of his chest muscles less obvious. Panther, Rayne's Jemhu bodyguard, was standing a little closer to Jock than normal, but Manhammer's rage, while palpable, was still fully under control. That was one of the most reliable things about the man.

"You will not be dissuaded, will you?" Jock finally ground out the words like lava oozing across the floor.

"That is correct," Rayne said bluntly.

"And what do I tell your father if something happens to you?" he asked, just as angry.

"That he should spend more time preparing cousin Zelda to the throne," Rayne snapped.

Honestly, if there was any way to put her cousin in her place, Rayne might have considered it, except that it would involve renouncing her place in the Royal Court, and all the perks that came with it. Not that Rayne hadn't considered it. Zelda would be a better Monarch.

What would Rayne do if she pulled this stunt off? Managed to actually penetrate the Forbidden Triangle and turn herself into something like a god? Would she want to return to a dowdy planet like Texas? Or would she find someplace more interesting to become the capital world of some new interstellar empire she might cause to come into being?

Shit, maybe she should just send the message to have Zelda replace her anyway. But that would be like burning her boats behind her.

Even as a Princess, Rayne had done stupider things in her time.

Jock's sour grimace spoke volumes, but King Zerik had assigned him the impossible task of keeping a headstrong daughter out of trouble, and here she was about to plunge headfirst into the greatest gamble she'd ever taken.

"I'll have Steffy with me," she nodded to the other woman.

Rayne was six feet tall in her stocking feet, and as

broad across the shoulders as most men, with the addition of hips, boobs, and still an enviable waist. Jock was still bigger. Steffy was Jock's height at six foot three, and weighed more than most men, the result of a lot of regular work with iron and all sorts of steroids and other chemicals making her body strong and hard.

Jock had assigned her the woman, because Rayne had wanted someone tough, rather than one of the petite ninjas that the Tantric Legion often turned out.

Steffy rose now, standing eye to eye with Jock. Almost as broad. Not nearly as mean, but nobody really was.

Like Rayne, she was dressed in combat boots, with pants tucked in, both in black. They had matching blue T-shirts underneath identical gray jackets, looking casual but capable of remaining dry in anything but a hard rain, and warm above freezing.

Steffy slung her bag over a shoulder as an exclamation point. It held two changes of clothes, along with knives, pistols, some food, and a few items that might be helpful, like a comm unit that Rayne didn't expect to really work when they got where they were going.

Assuming they did.

Rayne rose and shouldered her bag as well.

"If it gets really bad," she said in a voice that only Steffy and Jock might hear, "Dirk is on the ship. You could contact him and bring him up to speed."

"Bring Dirk Thruster in from the cold on this mission?" Jock sneered.

"When you find a better, harder, more dangerous man, Manhammer, you let me know," Rayne sneered right back, causing Jock to flinch now.

He was not Dirk's equal. Nobody was. At least Jock was smart enough to understand that and shut up now.

"I will try to send messages when I know where I'm going," Rayne said in a quieter voice, aiming to placate the man.

Nothing she'd ever done topped the insane stupidity of walking out that door with a complete stranger, hoping such a person would show her the greatest secret in the galaxy, just for the asking.

Rayne nodded at Steffy and walked to the door as though to her execution.

Hopefully, if a revolution ever came to Texas, she'd manage to remain as calm while being executed. As composed.

Really though, it was a good thing she'd already emptied her bladder and not had any coffee this morning, as Rayne wasn't sure she'd be able to hold it.

She emerged into the outer chamber, where six women in the pink and black uniforms of the Tantric Legion held guns loosely on a visitor who was not the least bit impressed.

The stranger was a woman of an indeterminate age that might be thirty-five, plus or minus fifteen years easily. Brown-red skin that looked Hispanic in origin, with black hair that had half-turned gray and white, but in beautiful stripes rather than layers. The skin around her eyes did not look loose and coarse, nor did she have crow's feet, but she still gave off the impression of great age. Shorter than Rayne, but Rayne was tall for any woman, and this newcomer was merely average. At least in height.

The stranger wore pants that covered her shoes and a

long, flowing tunic that was belted in place, with everything in a green soft enough to be olive. A floppy hat atop her head served more as part of a costume than a suggestion of impending weather, but the old psychic, Imelda, had warned Rayne to prepare for planetary conditions.

Which planet was yet to be determined.

The woman studied her now, a quick glance at Steffy that seemed to just confirm the woman as a witness and participant, rather than protagonist.

No, that would be Rayne. Princess Rayne of Texas. The girl who refused to grow up.

The weight of all those little choices settled on her shoulders now, but Rayne refused to be bowed.

"We are ready," Rayne announced, as if speaking the words would magically cause them to be the truth.

The woman smiled a little, knowingly, and inclined her head just the slightest bit.

"I doubt it, Princess," she spoke now, a higher voice than Rayne would have expected. Almost an operatic soprano, when her age might have suggested a deeper, almost mannish voice would emerge. "Come."

She turned and walked to the door without glancing back. Rayne nodded to her women and pasted a brave smile on her face when she looked at Jock, standing in the doorway behind her.

"Do you have a name?" Rayne asked as the woman triggered the hatch to open.

"Silia," she said, exiting into the corridor that would lead her to the lifts.

Other troopers were on guard now, but not as tightly

wound as the six in Rayne's chambers. The princess nodded at them and followed Silia. A lift had apparently been held, because the door opened as soon as the woman pressed the call button, and she entered.

Rayne and Steffy followed into the tiny chamber. She was close enough now to smell the woman, but couldn't detect any scent or perfume. Rayne had gone light this morning. Steffy had only her natural smell.

This other woman might have been a ghost.

She turned to glance at Rayne.

"Oh no, I'm quite real," she said with perhaps a ghost of a grin.

The lift doors closed and they began to descend.

JOCK WATCHED his princess exit and counted slowly, deliberately to ten before he spoke, knowing that the words would probably be irrevocably damning. But at this point, he figured he literally had everything to lose by remaining silent.

He turned to the closest trooper, ignoring Panther as that man faded into the shadows. The bodyguard who almost never spoke was just another pretty face around here, but the man would take orders from Jock, as long as they were geared towards protecting Rayne.

"Get Zamora in here," Jock said to the woman. He took a breath and cast the dice. "And someone find Dirk Thruster."

"Sir?" she asked, voice climbing.

"He's on the station," Jock said. "Zamora saw him and came that close to capturing him for us."

"But the princess said…"

"Damn what she said!" Jock yelled back, feeling his voice turn into an ugly snarl that could not be helped. "If we do end up needing Dirk, then we'll need him immediately. Offer him a complete truce so I can explain what's going on. The worst he can say is no and then we're back where we were before, but we'll know that much."

Bodies moved. Jock found himself alone, but that wasn't surprising, either, as his rage was vast and anyone remaining behind might become a target. Even Panther had withdrawn into another room.

Jock moved to the wet bar and fixed himself a drink, reminding himself that in space, it was always dinner time somewhere, regardless of his personal time being just after dawn.

This had a feeling worse than any of the other stupid things Rayne had talked him into over the years. Far worse.

Jock wondered if even Dirk Thruster would be enough to save her this time.

RAYNE FELT herself growing more nervous as the lift kept descending. There wasn't a space elevator that could take them to the planetary surface of Dr'Gonai, but she'd never appreciated just how many decks there were on the old *Sleeper Ship*.

How far down she could go.

A glance over at Steffy confirmed that the other woman felt it, too. Silia just smiled at the doors as if she was alone in here.

Rayne wanted to speak. To ask the woman questions, but held herself still and quiet, as far out of character as that was.

Was this growing up? Rayne had lost count of the number of people over the decades who had demanded it of her. Even Father had given up eventually, but he'd been too busy trying to be a good king while raising his only child, a headstrong daughter after Queen Aloisea had died.

Had it really been twenty-eight years since that day?

Rayne shivered at the passage of time and strove to breathe evenly. She would do this thing. Find out how to penetrate the Forbidden Triangle and that would be that.

Then what?

Rayne found that she had no idea what might come after that. She was shocked that she had even asked herself such a question. That was also well out of character for her, such introspection.

Or was it the fear speaking?

The little voice suggesting that the woman next to her might be a being of godlike power, just toying with her or testing her, rather than a simple guide. If there could be such a thing with the stakes as high as they were.

Again, she almost spoke. Almost demanded answers from Silia, but Rayne got the feeling that the woman might stop the lift, exit, and send her and Steffy right back to their former lives of mindless debauchery.

Rayne didn't want that.

Did she?

Just return to uncomplicated sex with interesting visitors, music and dancing all night, all the things that made the ennui of being a princess at least vaguely worth pursuing?

No.

Shit, no.

Rayne couldn't imagine even another week of such things, let alone a year. Better to let Zelda take the crown and become an itinerant mendicant than face one more diplomatic envoy wanting to talk about trade. Zelda wouldn't fuck everything up nearly as bad.

Rayne had a flash of sudden insight so hard it almost ripped her in half like some monstrous cock.

Dirk.

He'd been right on the verge of becoming a Timocrat, one of the ruling elite on Amaull, and had instead turned it down. Walked away into an alternative life of secret missions, martial arts contests, and sexual adventures.

He had chosen to give that other lifestyle up.

Jock had been washed out, but that was due to the temper underneath the man's hard facade. He had the brains to have passed, but not the emotional control.

Dirk had that. Had more than enough.

He had still become a wanderer.

Did she want that?

The lift hit bottom before she had an answer. The doors opened and Silia stepped out into a foyer for a flight deck, but not one Rayne had ever seen before. Several large bays lay beyond transparent walls, about half were fille with the tremendous freighters that flew constant circuits between orbit and planet, delivering all the food and supplies that the *Jira Sleeper Ship* needed to retain its legend as the 'Casino to the Stars.'

As a princess, she had always arrived via the VIP deck, up with the casinos and resorts, red carpet and gladhanding from her own, personal concierge, as a high-roller seeking only the most expensive, audacious holidays.

Yesterday, she had experienced some of the lower decks, which were really more just a small town that happened to be in orbit, rather than a seedy metroplex like she had always preferred.

Silia started walking without looking back. Rayne got the impression that failure to keep up with the woman going forward would be enough to be left behind, so she stretched her longer legs and closed the gap quickly, Steffy right on her heels.

They transited to the far corner of the front chamber, coming to a smaller bay that had a simple shuttle in place. Almost a bus, but not that big. Still, it had the feel of the vehicle that the lower deck folks used to go home for a quick holiday, when they couldn't afford the nicer transports

But then, Rayne was no longer the Princess of Texas, was she? She'd told Jock to get Zelda installed if she didn't come back.

Had she already decided not to return? Just on the flight down from the heavens of her penthouse to the hells of the lower decks?

Dirk.

She wasn't so arrogant as to think that if he could do it, she could. There was only one Dirk Thruster.

But he had showed her that it was possible to give up wealth and privilege, and find happiness instead.

Had she ever been happy?

No, not since Mother died. How odd that she'd never asked that question.

Already this quest had born fruit, and she had barely begun.

Who would Rayne Summers be tomorrow, if she was no longer a princess?

Silia keyed the hatch and entered the airlock, her two lost sheep in close pursuit.

The airlock began to seal with a hard beeping behind her, with the three of them trapped in between.

Rayne even wondered if anything bad would happen to Steffy, dragged along on this insane mission because Rayne had demanded a bodyguard who could intimidate men. This silliness was not something Steffy might have chosen herself.

But last night had shown Rayne sides of the other woman she would have never imagined.

Rayne had been so hot after letting Pretty Boy cum all over her tits while listening to Steffy phone sex the man to a hard, gasping orgasm. Then she got to watch Steffy lick up all that cum and offer the man a discount next time on a blow job.

Stopping in the stairwell afterwards so Steffy could lick Rayne's breasts clean, in spite of people walking by and complaining under their voices.

Then upstairs and into the shower…

There weren't many women in the Legion taller than Rayne. Or bigger. But Steffy had the natural height, and had supplemented her diet to let her grow mannish muscles under womanly curves.

They'd showered, nearly drowning a few times when one or the other had knelt to be able to lick all the places wet before the water had even started.

Then into the bedroom, with only Panther as a witness.

Those chemicals had indeed caused Steffy's clitoris to begin growing like a small penis, until it was a nub like the last two knuckles of Rayne's pinky. And Steffy enjoyed having someone suck on it like a cock, too, bucking and moaning that only got worse when Rayne had slipped two fingers inside her and began tapping on Steffy's g-spot in rhythm with her head bobbing.

Steffy's scream might have brought Legionnaires running, but they already knew what was happening in the room, and Panther had just watched enigmatically from the shadows, invisible but for his eyes.

That had gotten Rayne even wetter when they changed places and Steffy had started going down on her. Rayne remembered looking over and locking eyes with Panther. Golden-yellow eyes at the edge of the fire, like the predator he was.

She'd imagined him stroking himself as he watched her get eaten out. That big, black cock she had seen but never touched, uncut head appearing and disappearing as he worked the flesh beyond those spines. Rayne had stretched out flat, alone with Steffy between her legs like a hummingbird, but in her fantasy, Panther had walked right over to the side of the bed, cock still in hand but working faster now, eyes still locked on his goddess as he got closer and closer.

Closer and closer.

Steffy had reached up and pinched a nipple just as Rayne got to her peak, but in her mind, that jolt of tension had been Panther spraying his hot cum on her tits, just like Pretty Boy had done, covering her with his own lust as her orgasm had exploded with a scream that had left her throat a little raw.

Rayne caught her breath and fell back to the present, wondering what had triggered her to relive last night. Except that a quick glance at Steffy showed that the woman was also flushed. There was a scent of arousal around Rayne as the airlock finally sealed and the inside began to open. Hers or Steffy's, Rayne wasn't sure.

Rayne leaned over and touched foreheads softly with Steffy.

"Next time, I don't think I'll charge him," Rayne whispered to the woman.

"Hell, I might pay," Steffy chuckled back.

Maybe they needed to find the man and kidnap him, just to provide an audience and a hard cock to ride?

Rayne had always been something of an exhibitionist, but it had been impersonal, at a distance, flaunting her nudity and semi-nudity at people where all they could do was watch, rather than taking some complete stranger out onto a public catwalk so she could jack him off all over her breasts in front of anyone who happened to be watching.

But that had been the old Rayne. Yesterday. The new one was discovering sides of herself she'd never imagined.

Silia glanced over with a knowing grin and Rayne

wondered if the woman with them was a telepath. Was it possible that she'd been reading Rayne's mind, perhaps triggering these memories to see who Rayne really was?

Rayne shrugged and took hold of Steffy's hand for strength. The things she might be embarrassed by were failures where her own ambivalence and flightiness had brought her up short. Like yesterday when the old crone psychic had threatened her with pain and misery, just to see if she could cause Rayne to withdraw.

Old Rayne.

New Rayne was going to be an adventurer like Dirk Thruster, at least as much as possible. Maybe a nobody, but no longer trapped within the confines of expectations.

The airlock door was open now. Silia began walking, with Rayne and Steffy holding hands in her wake. It felt better this way, like she had a friend, rather than a big goon.

She had tasted Steffy, and been tasted. They had explored each other and enjoyed tender love as much as rowdy sex.

And now they were going to take a shuttle to the surface of Dr'Gonai and find her future.

Rayne found that even more arousing than the thought of a hard cock right now.

DIRK STOOD in the center of his hotel room and read the note again, still not believing it. Smelled like a trap. Shit, it even tasted like a trap. But Jock had included his personal guarantee of Dirk's safety, and Jock

Manhammer knew what that implied between the two of them.

Both Dirk and Jock had even read Plato in the original Greek, back when they were going to grow up and be philosopher kings. Jock was four years older, so Dirk hadn't really known the man all that well, back in those days. It had only been later, when Jock got recruited to command the Tantric Legion that their paths began to cross.

But Jock had always been an honorable man.

Fuck.

Dirk looked around his hotel room and grimaced. The soulless place wasn't as spartan as Dirk would have preferred, but he would have had to raise a stink to get that kind of service, and everything had been low key up until now.

For whatever good it had done.

Someone had slipped a note under his door without even knocking. Dirk had considered racing to the door and throwing it open, but hadn't felt like close combat, so he'd watched it for several seconds, letting whoever it was get away.

Then he'd read it.

Fuck.

Dirk opened his handcomm now and pressed a button.

"How may I serve your well-hung awesomeness?" Tiffany answered with a saucy lilt that suggested she was already on her knees, just waiting to see which way she needed to face.

"Come to my room immediately," Dirk said.

"I thought you'd never ask," she said, breathless with surprise.

"Not like that," he growled. "Bring a gun."

Dirk hung up before she could retort. The hotel had put her on the same floor, down three, so he rose and walked to the door, counting to six and then opening it as she approached.

Dirk nodded her in and looked both ways before closing. The hallways on this deck curved slowly, following the outer arc of the old ship's skin, letting people on this side have a porthole view of the planet below and the stars.

Tiffany entered and studied him. She was back to green skin, but had been purple when infiltrating the Tantric Legion earlier.

"You might need to revert to your normal form," he said as a beginning.

"What happened?" she asked, dialing down the raw sexuality as he watched.

Tiffany was stunning normally. The green skin and black hair didn't detract from that, but also didn't really do anything for him. He preferred the redhead version of the woman, truth be told, but now was not the time for a discussion of personal things.

"Jock Manhammer asked me for a meeting under truce," Dirk said. "Something has happened to Rayne that has him worried, but he won't discuss it except in private."

"Am I coming?" she asked, breathless.

Dirk glared at the double entendre, but she blushed instead of smirking.

"Sorry," she murmured.

"You'll be with me," Dirk said.

He studied her outfit and decided that it would work for now. She wore a top like a short sundress in dark blue, over leggings in dove gray. It made her green skin look almost fierce, like a forest dryad come to life.

Dirk was in simple black pants and a tan kimono top, held in place by a belt with various pockets, the thing being tunic length. He considered tucking a pistol in somewhere, but Tiffany would be armed, and Jock had his reputation to worry about.

They didn't have much, men like the two of them. Their word was at the top the list of valuables. Everything else was just in service of their own, personal missions. That he and Jock were vaguely-unfriendly rivals didn't change anything about the larger conflict aswirl around them.

"Now?" she asked.

Dirk nodded and opened the door, again looking both ways, but no ambush lay in wait.

It took time to transit the vessel to where Jock and the Princess were staying. Dirk walked quickly and Tiffany remained silent.

"Should we wake Rico up?" she asked at one point.

Dirk considered it.

"Probably," he replied, quickly typing a message into his handcomm and sending it. "That will ensure he has everything put back together, in case we need to fly somewhere in a hurry."

She nodded and kept up.

The last lift deposited them in a section of penthouse well removed from the big casinos, but still catering to the upper crust. If Dirk had any doubts about his location, the four women in pink and black uniforms, lower faces covered to hide identities and guns at the ready would have told him where he was.

He walked right up to the closest one, short and broad across the hips and shoulders, with dark eyes wide open right now.

"I'm expected," he said simply.

She nodded and gestured one of the other women through the door at the end of the hallway. That one returned a few moments later.

"It's okay," the second woman said.

"Go on," the first one nodded.

Dirk caught a hint of surprise in the eyes of the trooper in front of him, but she was looking at Tiffany instead of him, so Dirk wondered if this was Wendra he had heard about.

Tiffany fell in beside him as they approached the portal, and he could smell a hint of blush about the woman. He wondered what Wendra would say later, or if she would pretend nothing had happened. Tiffany had been purple at the time, after all. Might have all been a case of semi-drunken misidentification.

And pigs might fly.

They entered a salon that felt more like a place where people would be made to wait while Rayne got around to them. Jock was standing in a door to one side and gestured them to join him.

The new space was a large office configured as a meeting room. Dirk recognized the fourth person in here, the genderqueer agent who had almost been good enough to capture him before. He shared a nod and a smile with her as they all sat in four chairs around a low table covered over with a coffee service.

Jock looked up at Dirk and there was an impossible pain in his eyes.

"The Princess has disappeared," he said simply.

RAYNE LOOKED around the thing she thought of as a bus for carrying workers. Except that there was nobody aboard right now, with just the three of them in a space that could have carried forty easily. The outer hatch closed with another rattle of beeps to warn people, and lights were lowered from bright to late afternoon.

The cockpit door was visible at the front, but closed. There weren't even stewards standing around to serve.

Just the three of them.

Silia had sat in the second row on the left, where the bench was three seats wide. Rayne had slipped Steffy in to the window seat across from Silia, and then sat just across the aisle from the woman. Bags went into overhead bins and they hooked up belts for when the craft emerged from the bay and into zero G.

Around them, the ship continued to power up and the bay depressurized. It rose on repulsors and moved smoothly out into orbital space.

Rayne wanted to ask, "Where are we going?" but suspected she would be greeted with another enigmatic smile if she did.

"So now what?" was the phrase she settled for instead.

Ambiguous. Expectant without being bitchy or demanding.

Open to new experiences, whatever they might be.

"We have time," Silia spoke now, turning to look at her with a grin that almost seemed hungry. "The flight will take about three hours. I considered discussing philosophy with you during that period, but I've been listening to your mind and right now I'm too horny for rational discourse, so I'd like to fuck instead. How about you?"

Rayne blinked in surprise, wondering if she should be upset that the woman really had invaded her mind, but as she'd told Steffy, they might dealing with beings indistinguishable from gods. So, she rose to the challenge as they lost gravity and everyone began to float a little. Rayne unhooked her seatbelt and grabbed onto the seat back in front of her.

She studied the woman, still unsure if Silia was thirty-five or fifty, but it really didn't matter. Silia reached out a hand and Rayne took it, letting the woman pull her floating across the aisle like a balloon and into a quick kiss. Behind her, she felt Steffy turn to watch.

"Oh, you, too," Silia said, pulling Rayne across and holding her hand out to the tall woman now.

Steffy moved more awkwardly, but that might be nerves as much as anything. She'd been fantastic fun yesterday, once she relaxed enough to enjoy herself and Rayne.

Somehow, they all three ended up on a side, with the row of seats flat for sleeping but tilted. It would be an odd angle once they got to gravity, but Rayne figured they had an hour before then.

Steffy's impossibly long legs let her rise up and clamp onto the back of the seat in front of them. Not a passive observer right now so much as not immediately in the way as things got sorted.

Rayne considered the strange woman and the pulled her upright, with Silia locking her own feet under the bar below to hold her like she was standing upright in gravity. Rayne took advantage of nothingness to float, stretching herself out horizontal to the plane of the shuttle and walking around Silia with her hands, one hand on a hip for stability while the other crossed her stomach and caught.

She pulled herself against the woman's back now, pressing her breasts and hips and leaning in to kiss the woman on the back of her neck. Rayne used her teeth to pull the hat loose to float off, discovering that the woman had much longer black and white striped hair up there than Rayne had anticipated underneath it.

Steffy reached out a hand now and took one of Silia's, pulling it forward and letting it rest on her breast. The stranger began to knead it lightly, which seemed to be perfect, as both nipples stood up suddenly and Steffy gasped a little.

Rayne reached around and caressed Silia's breasts as well. The woman was smaller than her or Steffy, but aroused, as they were rigid points pressed into her palms. She licked Silia's ear and blew warm air in it as the woman began to hum quietly.

Movement caused Rayne to look up, but it was Steffy peeling off her jacket and shirt. Silia pulled Steffy close and went back and forth on the tall woman's breasts now with her left hand, while her right hand slid up and was rubbing her crotch.

That sounded like fun, so Rayne did the same to Silia, and got her first surprise.

"You have a cock," she whispered, feeling it grow harder as her fingers outlined it under the cloth.

"I have everything," Silia turned so she could kiss Rayne now, tongues meeting and dancing.

Rayne concentrated her senses on that cock as it hardened. It was bigger than Pretty Boy's had been. Possibly the same size as Dirk's, both for length and girth.

Rayne wanted to taste it, but there were too many clothes in the way. She let go long enough to remove her shirt and jacket, grabbing Steffy's floating gear and stuffing everything into an overhead bin. Silia turned and found a nipple as Rayne moved, one hand on Rayne's bottom to hold her in place while the other woman swirled a hot tongue over the sensitive skin.

Rayne just hung in space watching. Steffy moved now to hang with her long legs wrapped around Silia's thighs from behind, while her mannish hands caressed from chin to that hard cock tenting Silia's pants.

Silia began rubbing Rayne's clit now with a thumb, while her fingers traced the outline of Rayne's lips.

Rayne unhooked her pants and began to wriggle out of them as an excuse to escape before she came too quickly. It had turned into an adventure now. Yesterday jacking off pretty boy in public, and now fucking a complete stranger god on a bus.

Rayne floated to the ceiling and watched for a moment as Steffy got Silia's top off, revealing small, upturned breasts with aerola nearly scarlet, and pointed like mountain tops, most of the skin glacier-white from tan lines where she wore some sort of bikini top.

Nude, Rayne pushed herself off the roof and back down into the fray, diving headfirst.

Hands caught her and held her upside down with that cock in her face. Rayne opened the woman's pants and pulled it out, marveling. Just a little smaller than Dirk's, and the skin itself was more red, compared to his brown, but it smelled like life itself.

Rayne took Silia's cock in her mouth as someone pulled her thighs apart and began licking her pussy. She couldn't be sure who it was, but there was space, and three hands were suddenly exploring her. Rayne sucked, bobbing, uncaring as to who had just stuck a finger in her ass. Or who was sucking on her clit. It was all white noise pleasure.

At some point, a hand caught all her red hair in a fist and pulled hard. Rayne almost came right then, but lost her grip on Silia's cock in the process.

"Enough," Silia said gruffly, holding Rayne at arm's length in zero gravity and smiling. "If you keep that up, I won't be able to fuck you, and that's really my goal right now."

Steffy's mouth glistened, so Rayne assumed her friend had been eating her. Gods, that woman's tongue.

"What about Steffy?" Rayne asked, concerned that only two of them might peak, leaving the third to just take care of herself.

Utterly unfair of Rayne to be so greedy.

Again, that secret smile, like Silia was listening to Rayne's thoughts.

"In zero gravity, Steffy can ride my face while I fuck you, dear," Silia said simply. "When she's done, she can climb down and lick my pussy for a while."

"But you have a cock." Steffy was uncertain.

"You're a hermaphrodite, aren't you?" Rayne asked. "You have everything, you said."

"Indeed," Silia smiled. "I was blessed with two clitori for people to kiss at the same time, but right now I want one buried to the hilt inside you."

Silia pulled Rayne around and grabbed her ankles, parting them and dragging Rayne down until the hard cock was pressed right against her opening.

Gods, she was wet. Sopping. Deliriously horny, so she grabbed it and lined that spike up, impaling herself on it with her heels pulling around Silia's hips. She'd never done something like this without gravity. Everyone generally went out of their way to avoid freefall whenever possible, going so far as slipping out a flight bay so slowly that there was just a blip of uncertainty. This shuttle had no artificial gravity, but Rayne didn't know if they was Silia's choice, or the cheapness of the resort.

Didn't matter. Rayne was floating, fucking Silia hard, letting the woman's cock stretch her. Every ripple. Every vein. The way her head swelled out, like a ring to keep that cock inside her, every time Rayne pushed back.

Overhead, Steffy had started to climb onto Silia's face, but changed her mind and turned around so that she and Rayne were facing each other. Rayne's breasts normally hung low against her body, flat when standing. Almost the opposite of Silia's pointed cones. Steffy's were in between. Not large enough to hang, but firm.

Rayne reached out and caught Steffy by a hand, pulling the woman into a triangle where she could kiss her, one hand around Steffy's neck and the other feeling a nipple. Steffy liked hers pinched, but not twisted or pulled.

She watched the tall woman clench her thighs on either side of Silia's head and one of that woman's arms came up around her thigh to grip her ass and hold her in place.

Perfect triangle of pleasure, floating in space, rocking as Rayne slowed her mad thrusting and humping down so she could continue to kiss her friend.

Steffy's breath got shorter and sharper and she had to break the kiss, leaning away as her back arched and she started to spasm, so close that Rayne could practically taste the orgasm surging through the woman like a perfume someone had spritzed.

At the same time, Silia's cock seemed to widen and lengthen inside her, like a snake extending and holding her, pressing every direction and just filling her.

Silia also got spasmy and Rayne felt the orgasm building in the woman, just like it did a man, starting low and hard and causing them to just start jerking uncontrollably before they thrust forward as hard as they could to bury themselves in a welcoming pussy.

Rayne pulled Silia in deeper with her heels, feeling that cock just fill her up. Steffy hit a second orgasm, and that seemed to spark Silia. She reached down and a hand caught Rayne by the hip, almost painfully gripping to hold her.

That seemed to be what Rayne needed, because her orgasm hit just as she felt Silia empty her balls deep inside Rayne's overheated soul. Most men were good for a hard spurt or two, but Silia seemed to have a bottomless well of cum, flooding for as long as Rayne's orgasm went on.

RAYNE BLINKED. Had she actually passed out there for a moment? Steffy was floating free, tethered to Silia only by left hands interlaced. Rayne would have floated away as well, but Silia was still hard inside her and a hand caught hers.

She realized that she'd stopped breathing and started again.

"Wow," Rayne said, possibly the entire extent of her vocabulary right now.

"Yes," Silia agreed. "I needed that."

"I might have just died and been reborn," Rayne whimpered as Silia began withdrawing that lovely cock, leaving her feeling almost painfully empty.

"That happened yesterday, dear," Silia said, pulling Rayne up to float next to Steffy, before turning them both around and resting them on either side of her, three abreast and nude.

Rayne had been fucked completely out. Steffy might even be asleep, but Rayne could not.

"Yesterday?" she whispered to the woman.

Silia turned to her and smiled, breasts covered in sweat

and face gleaming where Steffy had cum her brains out while being eaten by this woman.

"We would have never bothered testing you otherwise, Rayne," Silia said in a voice that suddenly seemed as old as the universe.

We?

Test?

Rayne wanted to ask more, but darkness claimed her.

DIRK SAT BACK and absorbed the entirety of Jock's story, including the bits that probably weren't supposed to come up, but Jock had had a bad feeling about it all so he left it all on the table.

Dirk had that same gut instinct. This had already gone wrong, and was only going to get weirder and worse as time progressed.

Rayne had been set up, but none of the four of them could identify who. Professionals, though, to have known her that quickly and on sight, assuming that Rayne hadn't been skirting the truth when she told Jock that her name had never come up.

"What's your next step?" Dirk asked the man, sipping at the last, cold bit of coffee in his mug.

"She's in the field without protection," Jock replied, waving them off before anyone could speak. "Yes, Steffy is tough and big and capable, but she's one woman. The two of them could be overcome easily enough. That's just a factor of numbers or surprise. Slip them a Mickey Finn in their food or drink as easily as anything else."

Dirk nodded. Sound logic.

"Run me in the field?" he asked.

Jock nodded.

"If the two of you are willing," he said, gesturing to Tiffany. "The Timocracy obviously brought you in already, so this is just an extra layer. Plus, that puts as much of the Tantric Legion as I brought with me at your fingertips."

"Where's *The Libertine*?" Dirk asked. "*Longsword* is hidden on the planet below with Rico, but you can't do that with the big beast."

"A couple of systems away, also in hiding while the ladies commit some ground training in semi-hostile terrain," Jock nodded. "I'll send for them immediately if you think that would be good."

"I don't think it would hurt," Dirk agreed. "If only because that gives us more ships to give chase with, if we need to. If she's truly found a way to penetrate the Forbidden Triangle, I'm guessing that we'll have to contact the same people, or else we're stuck out here, hoping she survives."

"There's one other thing," Jock said, taking a deep breath. "I haven't mentioned it up until now, because I wasn't sure, but it might affect your decision making, Dirk."

"Oh?"

"She's seemed a little more moody than usual lately," Jock sighed. "Perhaps given to greater risks than before. I'm not sure what, but if she thinks I should contact King Zerik about preparing her cousin Zelda, I worry that she might be depressed on top of everything."

Dirk nodded. He'd wondered before if the princess

would reach a fork in the road where she either had to give up on all the crazy dreams of power she'd been pursuing, or double-down.

They might have arrived at that moment, which would just make everything all that much harder.

Dirk had always been able to count on Princess Rayne flinching at the last moment, when the stakes got too high. Now, she might leap instead.

He grimaced and nodded.

Zamona, on his right, was dressed in mufti rather than the pink and black uniform, but he already knew the woman was a field agent, rather than a trooper. She watched him with eyes that were interested, but not concerned.

Dirk tossed the dice in his head.

"Dress for the field," he told her. "Same gear they took. Meet us in my room in an hour and be prepared for being isolated in the field, because if we are successful, we're probably going the same place as Rayne and Steffy, and no communications probably won't work. Questions?"

"Why me?" Zamona asked in a quiet voice. "I failed earlier."

"You got much closer than most do," he smiled at her. "I pulled a dirty trick on you or things might have turned out much differently."

"Okay," she nodded.

Dirk rose and nodded at Tiffany. He shook Jock's hand and they were off.

Rayne might have finally gotten in over her head this time. He would need to pull her out.

DIRK OPENED the door at the knock, admitting Zamona in field clothing that had a paramilitary feel, but was also low profile in grays, with a bag slung over her shoulder. He and Tiffany had done something similar for clothing, but his gear had all gone into belt pouches and thigh pockets. One less thing to carry around, but not everyone approached things as he did.

Rico had been updated and was getting the ship back together from what he had pulled apart to fix, but they didn't need him immediately anyway. It was good enough that he would coordinate with Jock, possibly docking *The Longsword* into *The Libertine* on that forward flight deck that always felt like he was fucking the bigger ship when he landed.

Tiffany's bag looked more like an oversized purse, nearly a messenger bag, but contained a variety of gear and toys.

"Anyone need a potty break?" he asked the two women as Tiffany rose.

They shook their heads and Dirk led the way.

He'd gotten the whole itinerary from Jock, but skipped the coffee shop and went straight to the psychic, Tiffany and Zamona trailing by a bit as they walked, so he looked like he was alone and the two women gave off a vibe hopefully similar to Rayne and Steffy. Two women out exploring the station, and both could take care of themselves.

A chime announced him when he entered the shop by himself. A woman who matched the description of Imelda was already standing there behind a counter. Her smile was thin, but not cold.

Expectant, perhaps.

"How may I place you in my debt?" she asked in a high voice, heavy with inuendo.

"Folks are concerned about Princess Rayne," Dirk replied without preamble. "They asked me to investigate."

"She is gone," Imelda replied evenly. "Did you wish to pursue her?"

The woman placed an odd emphasis on the word *pursue*, but Dirk was used to people lobbing double entendres around him. Occupational hazard.

"Is she safe?" he asked.

Imelda shrugged negligently.

"She seeks a power and knowledge perhaps far beyond herself," Imelda said. "But she is still early on that road and might yet turn away from such introspection."

Again, such a strange vocabulary. It was like all the subtext of three conversations was being compressed into a single wafer for him to consume as part of a religious experience.

"And if she does not?" Dirk asked, flashing back to Jock's comments on depression and age maybe sneaking up on the Princess.

"We all take risks, Dirk Thruster," Imelda said, apparently knowing who he was without introduction. "Some prove minor."

"And others?" he pressed.

"They might cost a far greater amount."

Dirk grimaced just the slightest bit. The old crone was offering to perhaps rid the galaxy of Princess Rayne of

Texas, if he was reading her eyes correctly. Or at least turn her into someone else who was less of a threat.

He suspected that the odds of Rayne actually achieving whatever godhead might be available were so impossible as to be a rounding error.

But you might die in your sleep, or slip in the shower and break your neck. All life was risk.

"All life is risk," the crone said, seemingly echoing his words, if not just reading them out of his mind.

Dirk already suspected that this woman was far more than she'd appeared.

"We would see her safe," Dirk offered, letting the woman evaluate that as she would.

Rayne Summers was herself. She had set off on this mission for power, Dirk had no doubt. He and Jock worried that she might be taking too big of a risk. That nobody could save her, but in the end, she was a grown woman, responsible for her own decisions.

But she was not his enemy.

People who made an enemy of Dirk Thruster were not long in this galaxy.

This crone was not his enemy either, though she might bear some responsibility if something happened to Rayne. If so, however the was only culpable in the context of allowing it to happen.

She hadn't pushed the woman off the cliff, as far as he knew.

"We did not," Imelda spoke now, as if part of the conversation. Going on in his head. "She has chosen her steps at each stage. However, you are correct that this might be far greater than she ever envisioned. And the price much higher. Is it a price Dirk Thruster might pay?"

"I have already paid higher prices," he snapped at the woman, not angry but sharp. "And taken greater risks for my friends. I could have chosen the easy life of philosophical inquiry and debate, but that would not have made the galaxy a better place."

"And you think this might?" Imelda smiled now.

"I think that she does not know who or what you are," Dirk replied. "I don't know either, but the very fact that such knowledge exists tells me that there are those people who might kill to protect it. Or that they lay a trap for the greedy and unwary to tread, that such folks might be destroyed without ever understanding why."

Imelda nodded. Her eyes took on a different gleam now as she stared at him.

It was a look Dirk knew well, a woman wondering what he might be like in bed. Being past the first bloom of youth just meant that the skin was no longer as resilient to the touch. The breasts might have started to sag. Her vagina might not be as welcoming as the skin thinned and grew more sensitive in ways that could make penetration painful.

But there was so much more than mere penetration to the act.

Imelda licked her lips and Dirk wondered if he would be the price for them allowing him to go save Rayne. Or if the whole thing was a trap to draw in Rayne, knowing that other players would bring Dirk Thruster for them.

Had they set up a triple honey pot, when a simple invitation might have been equally sufficient?

"But we could not have known that," she murmured now, perhaps a touch apologetically. "Not until you were here."

"Is it already too late?" he asked her now. "For Rayne?"

"It is not, but she has gone on her own quest, and the dangers there are greater than she imagines," Imelda admitted.

"Then I must pursue and rescue her," Dirk stated flatly. "She is an innocent here, in spite of everything else."

Imelda nodded, bowing her head deeply to him.

On the one hand, that made Dirk feel better, that he was probably just dealing with a culture or species far in advance of his, and not true gods.

On the other hand, that also meant that they could fuck up, just like everyone else.

"Bring your two friends," Imelda said in a different voice now.

Harder. Deeper. More in line with the woman herself, if she was a demigod in drag.

Dirk nodded and stepped to the door to the shop, locating them across the way and gesturing Tiffany and Zamona to join him.

He turned back to find Imelda standing at the door to the back room. He followed her, the two women on his trail.

Surrounded by beautiful, dangerous women seemed to be his lot in life. Imelda might appear the ancient crone, but he could see in her face the young woman who probably stopped traffic just walking down the street on some planet.

What he didn't know was how many decades or millennia ago that might have been.

Imelda opened a door that had been hidden behind a curtain and pointed them into a corridor that was part of the back side of the station.

"That way," she said simply, pointing.

Dirk waved the two women through and paused, standing close to the old crone. Towering above her.

He leaned down and delicately kissed her when she didn't move away.

"Thank you," he said calmly. "Perhaps we'll have a longer and more meaningful conversation at some point."

"Perhaps," Imelda smiled that secret smile at him.

Dirk stepped through into another world.

DIRK HAD LET the women lead. The hallway was a long corridor that felt unnatural without any branching or even doors that they might pass. He even wondered if they were still actually aboard the *Jira Sleeper Ship*, since this corridor appeared to run beam straight, when so many of those others had a curve to them as they followed the outer hull inward.

The ship had been built almost like a fish, smooth and utterly unnecessarily streamlined in a way that served no other purpose in space other than to look pretty. But there was something important to be said there. Not everything had to be about brutal functionality and efficiency. In that case, every cargo ship would be a box with the exact same dimensions, holding so many standard containers in the tightest array possible for the engines.

No, he liked style and elegance that was expensive and occasionally silly to build and maintain. That was always how he thought of Humans.

Because it was there…

So he suspected that the door had been a portal. Nothing he was the least bit prepared to try to explain, save some vague hand-waving at science fiction tropes, but Dirk had a feeling that they had already shifted far beyond the sorts of things a rational scientist or philosopher-king might explain. But once upon a time, FTL had been deemed utterly impossible, too.

And he was Dirk Thruster, Man of Action. The guy who got weirder things than you in his breakfast cereal.

Dirk wasn't counting his steps, but he had a feeling that they'd already gone farther than the ship was long in this section, which that just reinforced his overall opinion. Tiffany had been following Zamona, and both women seemed to slow down by some unspoken agreement, so Dirk slipped between them to see what had caused them to pause.

The corridor was ending.

Dirk stopped and looked backwards, noting that the far end seemed to vanish into a nonexistent dusky haze in the distance, without any curve at all. He turned again and started off, walking closer to what was resolving itself into a hatch of a style Dirk wasn't sure he'd ever seen before.

Looking down, the floor had changed, from the extruded metal plates welded together with the smallest of seams to a diamond grate pattern raised just enough that a bare foot could feel it. Shinier, too, but Dirk didn't remember seeing it change.

The air was cooler, but not cold. Just a few degrees, but the difference between a shirt and a light jacket on a fall day. Some smell floated in the air, but Dirk couldn't immediately identify it, save that it left a hint of floral on his nose. Again, barely there, like the grid under his feet.

But different.

They had somehow *transitioned* between the *Jira Sleeper Ship* and here, wherever *here* was.

Imelda had said that her people might have made different choices, had they actually met Dirk, or thought to just send him an invitation.

This whole setup had taken to feeling like a tournament. Something he'd done numerous times, both for the martial arts as well as the tantric ones. Dirk had black belts and other colors of mastery from a number of schools and cultures, including one that was white with three yellow stripes, marking him as the second highest possible rank in that style, behind only pure yellow itself.

In the tantric arts, a black belt itself was a rare thing. His fourth degree made him one of perhaps only a dozen in the galaxy, all advanced students of the handful of true masters like Howie, who had originally trained Dirk.

He approached this door aware that he was somewhere else.

Dirk smiled. Weirder things in his breakfast cereal, but only some days.

He placed a hand on the latch handle that would apparently slide it sideways like a pocket door to disappear into the wall.

"Where are we?" Zamona asked quietly. Nervously.

But she was the Tantric Legion. Simple women, at the end of the day. Part of a paramilitary force organized by Rayne and serving under Jock. Just goons with guns in pretty pink outfits that made their asses look good.

A glance showed that Tiffany was emulating the great stoics, wrapped down tightly into herself in such a way that nothing and nobody was going to impress her all that much.

Not even gods.

Dirk smiled. He was prepared to meet such beings. To play a game of backgammon or fix them a gourmet dinner, as much as fight to the death.

He supposed that right there was probably the line that separated him from the rest of the galaxy. At least those folks still outside the Forbidden Triangle.

What interesting folks might he find inside? What kind of meals might he prepare?

How much fun was coming?

Dirk Thruster could not look upon his adventures as toils equal to Heracles. That would suggest a great weight on his back, a geas from the gods themselves.

To him, experiences were not chains but balloons, filled with helium to carry him over all manner of obstacles to see what might be over that next mountain.

"Deep breaths," Dirk told the two women. "We have arrived at the first blockage of what I suspect will be many, because the folks beyond wish to test our mettle and see how well we represent the Humans who are yet newcomers on the galactic stage."

Tiffany nodded. Zamona's was more jerky, but there wasn't much else Dirk could say to her.

Howie had summed it up best, years ago.

"I can't want this more than you do, kid," he'd said, grousing at the young punk come to learn how to seduce women and men with a smile. "Whatever it is. Find yourself. Then you can find everyone else."

Dirk nodded to himself and opened the hatch. The metal was cool under his hand, but warmed as he held it, like a cock hardening with blood on a chilly day. He flexed his taut back muscles and it slid away, leaving a six inch threshold to step over that took him into a room.

The air turned different as he entered. Blue, for lack of a better way to explain it, even as nothing changed.

Perhaps he was standing under a different star?

The room was a cozy salon. Fireplace on the far wall that looked like it was burning real wood, even as he saw stars out of the porthole on his right. Two chairs straddled the fire, old style wingbacks upholstered in purple and silver, with a sofa under the porthole.

A woman had been sitting in the chair on his left as Dirk entered. She closed the book in her lap and placed it on a side table, away from the flames and looked up at him.

He recognized the eyes as she smiled up at him, but she had changed.

Or perhaps this was what she normally looked like.

Dirk took a stride into the room and glanced back, not surprised that the hatch had vanished as if it had never existed, leaving only a wood-paneled wall with a starscape painted in oil.

She rose from her chair now and Dirk got to see what Imelda had looked like when she was young.

Amazing.

Her skin said twenty years old, but the eyes still looked ancient, dark with knowledge. All the wrinkles were gone, her skin now smooth and tight. Dirk's skin had a Mediterranean hue, a darker brown than many places, while hers had the redder hue of the western Americas, before the Anglos had arrived.

Loose black hair trailed down her back almost to her waist from the bits that flared to the sides as she stood.

She stared at him for another moment and Dirk took in all of her.

Elder crone had been thick through the middle with age, while this younger version had hard, upturned breasts outlined against a tight, thin sundress in a silver and purple that was the exact mirror opposite of the chair. It came nearly to her knees, but was a sheath she had been poured into like a poniard, rather than a series of flower petals held upside down.

Her hips weren't as broad as they would get when she got older, but her waist tucked in tight enough that he could see exactly where he would slip up behind her and grab the hipbones for leverage. And her legs had the look of a woman who had never once bothered shaving them.

Dirk found himself wondering what her pubic hair might look like in those circumstances. Or smell like.

She took a step forward as well now, until they were close enough to be two co-workers chatting in a hallway about last night's game. Imelda was barefoot and perhaps five foot four, a thoroughbred preparing for a race.

Dirk paused and sought something in those ancient eyes.

"So this is the first test?" he asked, wondering how many other gods might be circling them above and watching.

"It is," she said in that deeper voice she'd used just before he left her before, in the place he had to think of as the real world, at least for now.

Was he already inside the Forbidden Triangle?

"Only on the cusp," she said, shaking her head with a rueful smile. "You must still pass."

Dirk nodded and held out his left hand to the woman.

She took it and he stepped forward, still holding her right hand as he slipped his right around her waist and pulled her just close enough that they were now dancing without bodies touching. Imelda wore nothing he could detect under the sundress, but Dirk wasn't surprised. He just had to trace the cut and ripped muscles under her skin to know she was not necessarily Human, however reasonable a facsimile she might appear to be on the outside.

"Would it be allowed to kiss you?" he asked, focusing on her face now. On those exquisite cheekbones that age had once hidden behind bags and wrinkles "To pleasure you?"

Rather than answer, Imelda leaned forward and pulled his head down into a kiss, lips already parted and tongue just daring him. Dirk kissed her and pulled the woman the rest of the way against his chest until her breasts were pressed flat against his stomach and his thigh had slid partway between her legs.

Her kiss was like that first peach of summer, cool and moist and sweet on a hot day where you've been out in the fields baling hay by hand. Her hand came up now, resting on his neck and holding Dirk from withdrawing as they continued to kiss.

She broke it after possibly an eternity, leaning back a little in his arms to smile up at him from a nose away.

"How would you like to pleasure me?" she asked in a throaty tone.

"There are days I would have liked to have been a Nicia," Dirk smiled at her. "Just so I have four hands with which to touch you instead of two."

"Where else would you touch me?" she smiled.

Dirk flexed and realized that his shoulders had changed suddenly to the front/back configuration of that other species, with his upper arms around Imelda and his lower arms just dangling at his side. He found he could control all of them, so he reached out with his lower right and grasped her by the bottom, still covered by the sundress, even though it had ridden up a little as she had ground against his thigh. His lower left went around her neck and turned outward, combing through those thick tresses a few times as she purred.

Dirk took a soft grip on the third pass and pulled her head back a little. Not much, just enough that she arched her back, driving nipples into his flesh and riding his thigh now, grinding herself up and down as her clit made contact with the rough fabric of his pants.

He kissed her and continued dancing to music in his head, except that it began to play in the room now, the snaps of the fireplace somehow providing just the right rhythm section underneath.

Imelda ground her crotch against his thigh to the point that Dirk slipped his right foot forward to provide her an anchor. Imelda responded by lifting her leg and wrapping a heel around his calf, seemingly opening her up even more. She started to hum and groan a little into his mouth as he rocked her, his shoulders moving back and forth even as his grip around the woman provided an anchor as she dragged herself up and down his thigh muscles.

Again, eternity might have passed, but Dirk understood that none of this was real. Or all of it. Time might have no meaning at all where she had taken him, but that was fine, at least for now, as she was a wonderful interlude, as long as he could get back to the original quest to protect Rayne from whatever terrible thing she had stumbled into.

"It is not a trap," Imelda broke the kiss and said around gasps as he continued to rub her clitoris against his leg. Her pupils had dilated significantly and she blinked too much. "We built a machine to administer the test, to make sure that none of us allowed our personal feelings to intrude."

"Rube Goldberg?" he asked, leaning down and kissing her on the neck now.

That made her gasp and squirm more, so he continued.

"Perhaps," Imelda yelped as she seemed close to overloading on pleasure. "Complicated enough that almost anyone could be dropped into it for testing."

"Almost anyone?"

He nipped at her neck once, just closing his teeth without any pressure, but she groaned and seemed to almost melt, to the point that all four of Dirk's arms seemed to be all that was holding her upright.

"There are...certain—individuals who….COULD **not** be...evaluated—sufficiently," she gasped and stammered as he focused on locating every possible erogenous zone she might have, assuming that the answer wasn't just Imelda's entire body and mind at this point.

Dirk didn't answer her words, since he already suspected what she would say. Instead, he released his grip in various ways that he could turn the woman inside his arms and pull her back against him so she was facing the fire now.

He was hard. Rigidly pressed against her bottom now. One left hand went around her stomach to keep her from collapsing. Another took hold of her right hip and provided a fulcrum for his cock to press between the firm muscles of her wonderful ass and let her grip him with them. A third hand reached up and just cupped a breast, perfectly covering it and using all of his palm and fingers to massage all the way around it as she gasped. His final hand came up and touched the front of her throat like kisses from a kitten.

Imelda moaned and ground backwards against him. He could feel her heartbeat against his ribs as well as in her throat as he stroked the flesh.

He wanted her. Whether it was something in the air or just the fantastic element, he wanted to bury himself in her.

Dirk reached up and pressed her shoulder while holding her hip, so she bent forward. Two hands came to rest on the arms of the chair she had been seated in when he arrived. Two more hands reached back and caught him on the hips, so she was also a Nicia for this.

Dirk shifted things around without ever releasing her. His lower hands gripped her by the hips now, holding her in place now as his cock throbbed against her, just reaching her clit with his tip when he pressed forward. One hand took hold of her hair, right at the base of her skull, and gripped. Not pulling. Just anchoring her in place.

Dirk reached down and caught the silky material of her sundress in a hand that pulled it up until her bottom was exposed. No tan lines, but he wasn't surprised, as she could appear however she wanted, and that tone of skin barely tanned in the sun.

It was one of the most perfect bottoms he thought he had ever encountered, in a lifetime of being an ass man. Chemistry and surgery could give a woman any breasts she desired. Any hair. Even change her skin tone on a daily basis. But the ass took a lot of work. Focus.

Dirk had known a woman who was utterly homely to look at. Just plain ugly. Flat-chested, too, with no curves worth mentioning. Instead of bemoaning her fate, she had walked and lifted, and had an ass that would stop traffic in the right dungarees, until she'd found a man who got past the face and realized who the woman underneath was.

Dirk remembered her, but right now he wanted more of Imelda than to just witness the perfection of her bottom. He let go of her hair and pulled the sundress off both shoulders now.

Imelda responded by holding his thighs tighter and hanging out into space as she wriggled her arms out of the dress, leaving it like a thick belt around her waist, but he wanted all of her.

Dirk gently tugged the cloth as they both adjusted hands and grips, until it puddled at her feet, relaxing his pressure everywhere until she was just standing there, proudly presenting her bottom to him.

Dirk took a moment to think about it and found himself nude without any remembrance of disrobing. His cock, freed, stuck out like a flagpole from the side of a building.

As much as he wanted the just step forward and hammer it into the woman mercilessly, he held back. Pulled at her shoulders until she was mostly upright again, her pussy sliding back and forth on his cock as she straddled the hot iron rod between her legs without ever slipping it inside.

It wouldn't take much. She was soaking wet with desire, her lips clenching at his cock like fingers, but too slippery to hold it.

His four hands were on both her hips, keeping her from escaping, as well as her breasts, demanding them by the way he kneaded the tissue lightly and worked her nipples. Her smell had grown heavy with musk and desire, filling the room with *need*.

But Dirk was still wanted more. One inner hand went lower, encountering a bed of pubic hair that had never been trimmed, running seeming forever across her groin and hips, down her naked thighs, so he traced both legs to her knees now, bringing his hands back up the inside of her spread thighs though the thick hair that wanted to hold him.

Up and then inward, until the base of each thumb encountered her labia, pressed outwards by the way she was seated astride his cock. He rubbed the sides of her clit with the backs of his thumbs. Her moaning turned into squeals of delight and desire, wriggling against his hands, cock, and stomach, so Dirk worked just her sensitive spots, at the same rhythm as her pussy was sliding forward and backwards on his cock.

So many women trimmed or waxed down there in the modern era that it was rare to encounter that sort of thing as he explored her hair. To Dirk, it was almost like an encounter with a primordial goddess, a poor man come to a primitive, roadside temple and praying, only for the Goddess herself to come down and offer herself to him. The hair around her pussy was as thick as on his chest, which just compounded the feeling.

He bent down to kiss her neck now and she had an orgasm. Rocking and clutching at him. Moaning that turned into whimpers, even as six of the eight hands involved held her in place between his hips and the chair while two of his continued rubbing her clit.

"In me," she gasped now. "Please."

Dirk released his iron grip and slid backwards now, even as she had a second orgasm from the change in pressure. He pushed her torso back down until her ass was presented, and then slid forward slowly, letting her guide him into her pussy, even as they held on with lower arms.

She was like fire inside, but her muscles were relaxed, so he went in all the way to the hilt on his first thrust. That triggered another orgasm on her part as she let all her weight go forward onto the arms of the wingback chair.

Imelda began to push back, even as he started to withdraw, so Dirk just held his cock still, buried inside her. One hand traced down her spine lightly while the other got hold of hair and pulled just enough that she exploded again, two hands on the chair, one on her clit, and another tracing her neck.

Dirk wondered how many times a goddess could come in a row before she passed out from the pleasure. There were limits to mortal flesh, after all, but this woman had probably never been Human to experience them.

Her cries of pleasure almost seemed to make the fire itself dance, so fiercely she was screaming now.

Dirk withdrew his cock, but he had to actually push her away from him to gain even an inch. As soon as he relaxed, she practically slammed him into her again.

He wondered if this being had ever fucked like this before. Been fucked bent over the arms of a chair. Had her pussy stretched, from the way those muscles clamped down on him now.

But she relented after a second, letting him start to pound her. Imelda didn't seem to want anything but a brutal pile-driving of a fuck right now, so he skipped all the other parts that might come in first. The kisses. The caresses. The various positions, geometric or gymnastic, that they might explore to build the tension and the sensitivity of skin.

The Goddess needed his cock, and Dirk wasn't sure he'd be able to stop if he wanted.

Fontunately he didn't want to stop.

He wanted her. The smell of her was driving him mad with desire. With the need to fill her pussy with his juice and his power, like the ancient legends of the male sky god impregnating the earth goddess to create the world.

A tiny portion of his mind wondered what Creations or Creation myths he was in the process of seeding now.

Her cries and orgasms had not so much as paused as he continued to fuck her, but Dirk had lost track of the number now, except as her vagina alternatively grabbed and stroked his cock inside her as he pumped.

Dirk finally caught fire, at least in his mind. His eyes were closed so he could not be sure if he would find the two of them engulfed in a corona of flames were to open them. All that existed were the roars of her pleasure and his need to fill her with a bottomless sea of cum.

The fire took root in his mind and traveled slowly down Dirk's spine to reach his anus and climb inside, lighting his prostate with napalm.

Dirk wondered if his cock had turned to solar plasma from the way it seemed made of molten steel now. All his muscles clenched except his heart, beating so wildly that nothing could contain it.

He erupted, leaving bruises wherever he touched her flesh and pulled her against him. Oceans of creation to fill the Goddess with his seed.

Her orgasms had not relented. But she seemed to draw power from his, and her cries presaged the birth of a new universe, spun off from this one by the immensity of their fucking.

He couldn't call this love-making like he would normally undertake with a new partner. This was raw fucking. Hot, hard, powerful, indomitable. He pumped her full of cum.

A supernova destroyed the universe.

———

DIRK OPENED his eyes and found himself in a room of rough metal walls that reminded him more of the *Jira Sleeper Ship* than where he had just been. Smooth floors. Old steel walls with hints of rust in places.

The air smelled clean and sweet, but had a hint of mold behind it, like water had seeped somewhere and created rot.

He was dressed, but flushed, as if from running.

Two arms instead of four, which suddenly just weren't enough.

He drew in a breath and heard a gasp behind him.

Turning, he found Tiffany as she had been when he first saw her at Hazeldale. Her face was flushed red with exertion, but she was back to being a redhead, with hair just a little longer than a bob.

"Did that just happen?" she asked in a tiny voice.

"Probably," he replied, unsure what she had seen and done but confident that it had not been that different from his experience. Perhaps instead of Imelda she had met a primitive war god and defeated him with her pussy.

Tiffany's body was amazing, from any angle you wished to explore.

He looked around, but it was just the two of them.

"What about Zamona?" she asked.

"Apparently, she failed the test," Dirk said, wondering.

Most likely, the test had been to reach deep into your soul and tap the endless well of sexuality every person had. Zamona had probably sought to hold back, or been unable or unwilling to give of herself, but Dirk wasn't all that surprised.

Assassins can never truly expose themselves to others.

A sound caused Dirk to move to a defensive crouch. A door in one wall opened, letting daylight from a planetary surface in, along with a light breeze.

"What the hell?" Rayne gasped as she stopped herself halfway through the door.

He had the impression that she had somehow also reverted to herself from some other image, but Dirk had no way of guessing what disguise the Princess might have undertaken.

Behind her, Dirk saw a second woman, bigger than most men, but he had been expecting that. Apparently both Rayne and Steffy had passed their carnal test.

He wondered what the next one would be.

"Dirk?" Rayne cried. "What are you doing here?"

"We came to help," he said.

"So we're on the right track?" she said with excitement. "We'll be able to get home?"

"I don't know," he said. "That wasn't exactly what they promised us. I suspect that this is all part of a larger test of who you are."

"But you'll be there to help me?" Rayne asked, quieter now. "I feel like this has gotten bigger than anything I imagined it would be."

Nervous. Maybe even a little scared from her tone. Jock had suggested that she might be depressed on top of everything else. Might be ready to leap blindly off a cliff, when she had always stopped herself short.

And they were all inside some sort of automated machine now. A Rube Goldberg contraption designed to *test* a human.

"I'm here," Dirk promised the woman. Women.

That was as much as he could honestly give them right now.

Be sure to pick up all the Dirk Thruster stories!

Volume 1:
Dirk's Secret Mission
Jira Sleeper Ship
Tantric Legion
Princess of Texas
Rayne's Quest

Volume 2:
Steffy
Jungle World
Transformations
The Law

Available now!